Luisa in Realityland

Other Books by Claribel Alegría:

Fiction

Tres Cuentos
El Detén
Album familiar
Pueblo de Dios y de Mandinga
Luisa en el país de la realidad

Poetry

Anillo de Silencio
Suite
Vigilias
Acuario
Huésped de mi tiempo
Via Unica
Aprendizaje
Pagaré a cobrar
Sobrevivo
Suma y Sigue
Flowers from the Volcano
Poesía Viva
Petit Pays
Poema-río

In Collaboration with D. J. Flakoll

New Voices of Hispanic America
Cenizas de Izalco
La Encrucijada Salvadoreña
Cien poemas de Robert Graves
Nuevas Voces de Norteamérica
Nicaragua: La revolución sandinista
No me agarran viva: la mujer salvadoreña en lucha
They'll Never Take Me Alive
Para romper el silencio: resistencia y lucha en las cárceles

LUISA
IN REALITYLAND

by
Claribel Alegría

translated from Spanish
by
Darwin J. Flakoll

CURBSTONE PRESS

for Carol

first English language edition: 1987
printed in the United States by R. R. Donnelley & Sons
cover design: Stone Graphics

This publication was supported in part by
donations made by private individuals and by
a grant from the Connecticut Commission on the Arts,
a state arts agency whose funds are recommended
by the Governor and appropriated by the
State Legislature.

LC: 87-71705
ISBN: 0-915306-70-0 cloth
ISBN: 0-915306-69-7 paper

distributed in the U.S. by:
The Talman Company
150 Fifth Avenue
New York, NY 10011

Curbstone Press, 321 Jackson Street, Willimantic, CT. 06226

Luisa in Realityland

WILF (1)

"Don't tell a soul, but tomorrow I'm leaving this place," Wilf confided to Luisa at the end of her gym class.

"Where are you going?" Luisa was startled; after all, she was only seven.

"I don't know yet. You have to keep the secret for three days; after that you can tell your parents."

Luisa began to pout.

"Come, come, don't do that. You'll see that we'll meet again. Take a good look at me. After age 40 a person doesn't change a whole lot. If some day you think you recognize me, just come up and say, 'I'm Luisa,' and I'll open my heart to you."

Wilf had arrived in Santa Ana the year before, Luisa recalled. He was on his way to Brazil to accept a position as professor of philosophy at the University of Sao Paulo, but during the voyage he fell in love with Aunt Olga, who was returning from Germany after two years of schooling there.

The folks of Santa Ana had never seen the likes of him. Two weeks after his arrival, he asked Luisa's parents to invite some friends and family over the following Sunday so he could recite passages from Faust for them in German.

"The only one who understands German around here is Olga," Luisa's father attempted to defend himself.

"That makes no difference," Wilf replied, and he turned up punctually at 9 p.m., clad in black tie and tails.

The patio corridor was illuminated only by candle light, just as he had instructed. Olga's family and friends took their seats while Wilf, with measured pace, dishevelled hair and pursed lips, made his way to the podium, which was also illuminated by a single candle.

Even before he began reading, the entire audience, save for Luisa's parents, was convulsed with laughter. Luisa listened, fascinated, from a corner, and Wilf fixed his eyes on her and occasionally gazed sadly at Aunt Olga.

That same evening he offered to give the little girl classes in Latin, Greek and gymnastics. He spoke something like 20 languages, but nobody believed him until one day a group of Santa Ana professionals and businessmen organized a banquet at the Hotel Florida to show him up. They invited a Frenchman, a gringo, an Italian, a German, a priest and a Greek. They even invited a Turk. While they were still on the first course, each of them began speaking to Wilf in his own tongue, and according to Luisa's father (there were only men at the banquet, of course), after he had finished speaking to all of them, Wilf began addressing each one in his own language, not the way it is spoken today but as it was spoken in the olden times. They were all stupefied, and after that they treated Wilf with more respect, except for Aunt Olga, who always stood him up and who started going around with a rich kid who had a flashy sports car and who invited her to Lake Coatepeque every Sunday to go cruising in his speedboat.

THE CEIBA

How was my ceiba?
the one facing the park
the one to which
I made a promise?
I remember it
as a shadowed roof
as a gigantic pillar
sustaining the sky
as the sentinel
of my childhood.
Beneath its thick branches
each of them like a trunk
the street sellers
rested
children and dogs
scampered about
the air paused
to watch us.
My absences
have been lengthy
innumerable
lengthy
but they never weighed on me
like now.
I still must return
the final station
is always the hardest
weariness accumulates
dismembers us.
How was my Ceiba?
I sense your map
in its foliage

the circle is open
I must still return
to close it
the trunk of the ceiba
is thick
cannot be encircled
with an embrace
I have made many trips
around it
many slow circles.
They won't let me return.
Hostile forces
forbid it.
Just one last circle
to close the ritual
one last return
to arrive at my Kaaba
and sit in the park
to contemplate it.

LUISA'S LITANIES

Every night before falling asleep, Luisa prayed an Our Father and an Ave Maria. At the end of her prayers she asked a grace for the souls of her dead grandparents. "Never forget to ask grace for them," her mother told her. "The dead need to be remembered and to be named so they don't fall into limbo."

Luisa was deeply impressed with the idea of limbo. Every time some relative or friend of the family died, she began asking for them. After that it wasn't only her friends and members of the family, but also the authors of her favorite books. It didn't matter if they had died a long time ago, like Miguel de Cervantes, or more recently, like Stefan Zweig, who, to make things worse, had committed suicide.

The increasing number of the dead began to weigh on her: Mama Chabela, Mama Clara, Papa Manuel, Alfonso, Uncle Pastor, René, Elsa, Aya, Arnoldo, little Alejandro, Stefan Zweig and Mrs. Zweig, Porfirio Barba Jacob, Rabindranath Tagore, Miguel de Cervantes y Saavedra, don José Luís Méndez, José Angel, and on and on. Once somebody was added to the list, Luisa kept naming that person night after night, and if, accidentally or out of sheer fatigue, she forgot someone, she would wake up later with her heart pounding.

The problem was, what could she do to keep the list from becoming endless? From now on, she promised herself one night when she was on the point of exhaustion and had just added to her list the name of Sinforoso Reyes, who had died by swallowing cyanide, I will only add the names of my parents, my brothers and sisters, Mama Nela, Papa Lico, Chus Ascat, Chabela, Angela, and of course, anybody who commits suicide.

13

WILF (2)

"It's strange that Wilf hasn't dropped by today," Luisa's father said at the dinner table. "He hasn't turned up for the past two days."

Luisa knew that she was growing pale, but she contained herself and nobody noticed.

"That's true," her mother said, "he hasn't so much as telephoned. Maybe you should drop by the hotel; he may be ill."

"After what happened the other day," her father grinned, "I wouldn't be surprised if he'd left town without saying goodbye to a soul."

It had occurred to Wilf to call on Ricardo, Luisa's uncle, dressed in a Scotch kilt. That did it. He set the whole town in an uproar, and small boys followed him down the street, throwing rocks at him and shouting "Fairy! Queer! Nya-a-a!" The poor man was pallid by the time he reached her uncle's house, stumbled inside and demanded a glass of water.

"Savages!" he exclaimed, perspiration streaming down his brow while the kids kept throwing rocks at the front door. "This is a town of savages!"

"I'm worried," her mother went on. "Something must have happened to him. There was an item in the paper today about an unidentified man's body being found in a *finca* near Juayúa. I don't know why I thought of Wilf."

"Don't be silly," her father said. "He told me some time back he was looking for work. That corpse must be of someone who was fleeing arrest. Martínez has issued orders to shoot all suspicious persons on sight."

"Horrible things are happening," her mother sighed, "and Wilf speaks his mind, no matter who's listening. Probably the *Guardia* has him under observation."

14

"Nature doesn't forgive!" Luisa recalled Wilf thundering the day after the massacre in Izalco.

"Where on earth can he be?" Luisa's father wiped his lips with his napkin. "The truth is, I like him. I'll stop by the hotel and see him tomorrow."

"Maybe he just wants to be alone," Luisa ventured.

"Isn't it strange that he bought Luisa all those valuable gifts?" her mother frowned.

Almost a week before, Wilf had appeared with three gifts: a green porcelain teacup with gold incrustations from Japan, a necklace of cultured pearls with a sapphire clasp, and a book of reproductions of paintings by 16th century German artists. "These were things of my mother's," he said, "and I want Luisa to have them."

Her parents protested in vain. "I don't like to carry superfluous things around with me," he overrode their objections.

"It's as though he were stripping himself of everything he owns," her mother said.

"He leads a completely ascetic life," her father agreed.

Luisa felt she couldn't hold back her secret much longer and asked permission to go to bed without dessert. The last thing she heard as she left the dining room was her mother musing. "Don't you think he might be the Wandering Jew?"

UNTIMELINESS

Sometimes
I think of you
of what might have been
of your tenderness trapped
of untimeliness.

LUISA AND THE GYPSY

Luisa and the gypsy girl were close friends. Ever since Luisa was very young, the Gypsy appeared in her dreams, and the two of them would undergo incredible adventures. At the beginning, Luisa was frightened, because the Gypsy was terribly daring and got her into all sorts of scrapes. Luisa never forgot the night the two of them visited a market place that had an Oriental atmosphere, and the Gypsy talked her into stealing three or four necklaces of colored beads and some gold-plated bracelets. The owner of the jewelry stall, who had long black hair and who was wearing pantaloons and a blouse embroidered in lilac thread, chased them through innumerable labyrinths. Luisa woke up screaming and swore that she would never steal anything again.

The Gypsy was impatient with her fears and sometimes spent months without visiting her. At one point, several years went by. That was when it occurred to Luisa to start having children. "You've turned stupid," the Gypsy told her. "You aren't the least bit interesting any more."

They renewed their friendship when Luisa started painting. She reappeared suddenly with her loud skirts and her long earrings. The Gypsy encouraged her to keep on and started dictating love poems to her. Since she was illiterate, she had to dictate them to Luisa who, as soon as she woke, would write them down in a special notebook she kept by her bedside.

I LIKE STROKING LEAVES

More than books,
magazines
and newspapers,
more than mobile lips
that repeat the books,
the magazines,
the disasters,
I like stroking leaves
covering my face with leaves
and feeling their freshness
seeing the world
through their sifted light
through their greens
and listening to my silence
that ripens
and trembles on my lips
and bursts on my tongue
and listening to the earth
that breathes
and the earth is my body
and I am the body
of the earth
Claribel.

WILF (3)

We never saw Wilf again. Whenever Luisa travelled she would look attentively at all men of 60 years or older. His features were difficult to forget, and she was certain that even though many years had gone by, she would recognize him.

Aunt Mercedes, Olga's sister, thought she saw him once in Mexico.

"It was in front of the Soviet Embassy," she told them excitedly. "He walked out of the entrance with a black velvet cape over his shoulders. I shouted, 'Wilf!' and he turned to give me a long contemptuous stare before he climbed into a black limousine that was waiting at the curb."

Who were you, Wilf? Nature has yet to claim its revenge.

AUNT ELSA AND CUIS

What on earth could have happened to Cuis?" Mama Chon was turning the house upside down in her search for the little animal. "He was here just a while ago." She peered sharply at Luisa. "Are you sure you shut the door tight when you came in?"

"Yes," Luisa nodded. "I played with him a bit, but then he crawled back under the sofa."

"Poor little thing," Mama Chon sighed. "He hasn"t been the same since Elsita died."

Cuis was an 8-year-old Dachshund. His passion was to hunt flying cockroaches, and he would leap high in the air to snap at them.

"It's incredible how high he can jump," Elsa would laugh, "with those stubby little legs of his."

Aunt Elsa couldn't have children, and her husband brought Cuis home for her when he was a two-week-old puppy. Since he had been weaned prematurely they had to bottle-feed him. He slept in a basket lined with cushions and hot-water bottles.

When Aunt Elsa fell ill he refused to leave her side except to trot out to the patio to perform his necessities. He ate beside her bed, and despite the doctor's recommendations, she hid him beneath the sheets and he slept at the bottom of the bed.

"She prefers him to me," Rodolfo muttered darkly. He didn't realize the seriousness of his wife's illness.

Cuis, on the contrary, knew perfectly well that something was terribly wrong. Three days before Elsa's death, when she could no longer speak because the croup had closed her throat, the little dog refused to leave her for a moment. Instead of jumping from the bed as he always did when the doctor arrived, he crawled down to his mistress' feet and lay there quietly.

"Her condition is extremely grave," the doctor told Rodolfo that morning. "She has entered a semi-coma."

Cuis crawled up to the head of the bed and licked his mistress' face.

"That damn dog!" Rodolfo exploded and pushed him to the floor. "Why don't you take him home with you?" he asked Mama Chon.

She took him with her that day and kept him enclosed in the house.

When Elsa died in the Polyclinic three days later, Cuis seemed to sense what had happened. He refused food for 48 hours. During the folowing weeks, he spent most of the time under the sofa, and no matter how many flying cockroaches buzzed through the corridor, he refused to move.

"You'll have to go look for him around the neighborhood," Mama Chon told the cleaning maid.

"I already went all over, and no one has seen him," the maid replied. "If a car had run over him, somebody would have told us."

"How very strange," Mama Chon said, "it's the first time he's run off." She busied herself calling the dog pound and placing telephone ads in the newspaper, offering a reward.

The following day the little dog still had not reappeared. Mama Chon and Luisa went to the marketplace to buy flowers for Elsa's grave on the first monthly anniversary of her death.

"It's terrible how the weeds spring up," Mama Chon grumbled as they approached the tomb, "I'm going to have to change gardeners."

The family mausoleum stood a long way from the entrance to the cemetery, and it looked much like all the others. It was crowned by a cross of white marble, with an angel perched atop the cross. Luisa ran ahead to open the iron gate.

"Mama Chon! Mama Chon!" she shouted, "Look who's here."

On the wilted flowers, above the very spot where Aunt Elsa had been buried, lay Cuis, rigid in death, his four small paws raised toward heaven.

I'M A WHORE; ARE YOU SATISFIED?

When Luisa was ten years old her mother decided she should learn to play tennis. Three times a week at 5 in the afternoon she went to the Modelo Park, which boasted the only tennis court in Santa Ana. Carlitos accompanied her. He was the son of her parents' best friends and a neighbor for many years.

Carlitos was several years older than Luisa. He took communion every Sunday, was the best student in his class and had a face full of pimples.

Invariably, before they left the house, Luisa's mother would say, "Take good care of her, don't let her forget her racket, remember she's terribly scatterbrained, and don't dawdle anywhere. I want you back here by 6:30 on the dot."

One afternoon, when they had played for more than an hour and were returning sweatily and in silence, Luisa suddenly stopped before a door that was always left standing ajar. A bead curtain prevented anyone from seeing who was inside.

"What are you doing?" Carlos asked.

"Nothing. It's the only door I've seen with a curtain like that."

"It's a whorehouse."

"Don't use dirty words," Luisa scolded him, as she separated the hanging strips of beads.

"If you don't come along, I'll tell on you." Carlos started walking away.

Luisa hesitated. Whore was a bad word. Whores were bad women. She shivered slightly, and just then the curtain opened.

"What do *you* want?" a woman in a pink dress asked bitterly.

Luisa's heart skipped a beat.

23

"If you don't hurry up, I'll leave," Carlitos called from the corner.

"Nothing," Luisa told her. "It's just that I like your curtain."

"Run along and stop bothering."

"Are you bad?" Luisa felt her legs trembling.

"I'm a whore; are you satisfied?"

"I'm going to tell your father," Carlitos shouted.

"May I see what your house is like?" Luisa asked.

"There's nothing to see," the woman said, pushing the curtain wider.

Luisa entered slowly and cast her eyes over the room. A pungent odor of disinfectant filled her lungs. Above the cot, a silver plated Christ gazed down at the floor. Chromo saints hung on the walls, and there was a shelf with the photograph of a young boy and a vase of artificial flowers.

"Are you satisfied?" the woman asked in the same bitter tone.

"If you were bad, you wouldn't have so many saints on your walls," the little girl said.

The woman burst out laughing.

"Who told you that whores are bad?"

Luisa didn't answer.

"Would you like a caramel?"

Luisa nodded yes.

The woman walked over to the wardrobe painted blue and took out a jar filled with candies.

"Help yourself," she said.

Luisa selected one.

"Take some more."

"I'd like to be your friend," she said as she chose three more.

The woman smiled.

"You'd better run along." She placed the jar on the night table that was also painted blue. Her tone was no longer bitter, and her gaze was softer.

"How old are you?" she asked.

"Ten."

"That boy you see there," she aimed her chin at the shelf, "would be twelve now. He died of dysentery."

Luisa felt like hugging her, but contained herself.

"Run along now," the woman placed a hand lightly on her shoulder, "and don't tell your mother you've been here."

Carlitos was waiting at the corner.

"You're stupid," he said. "That woman is a whore, and whores are bad."

"You're the one who's bad," Luisa retorted, and she began running toward her house.

TROPICAL BIRDLAND

I wanted to be a *chiltota*
a *clarinero*
a *zenzontle*
but I'm only a buzzard
with stubby wings
who limps through time
wasting away.

26

THE ANCESTOR ROOM

"Since Laura and her family are away on a trip, we're going to her house to visit my sister," Chabe told Luisa one day when they were returning from the market.

Laura was the same age as Luisa, and they were close friends. Luisa's father was the family's doctor, which was undoubtedly the richest in the entire country. Laura's grandfather had been president, and she had a Swiss governess and two Pekinese dogs. During school vacations the whole family travelled to Europe, where they had houses in Germany and France and a real castle in Switzerland.

"Hello," Lipa greeted them, happy that her sister had come to visit her. Lipa had been the family housekeeper for years and years.

"Why is all the furniture covered?" Luisa asked.

Lipa laughed.

"To keep everything from getting dusty."

Luisa repressed a shudder as her eyes roved over the salons where she had so often played with Laura. The covers seemed like funeral shrouds, and the portraits of Laura's ancestors, painted by European artists, stared down at her in a very strange manner.

"Don't touch anything," Chabe warned her. "You'd better come with us to the kitchen."

Luisa obediently followed the two of them.

"Would you like a refreshment?" Lipa asked her as she opened the enormous refrigerator. The three of them sat around a table in the pantry.

"This is awfully good." Luisa savored her *guayaba* punch. "Aren't you afraid of staying here alone, Lipa?"

"I'm not alone," the other smiled at her. "Carmen and her daughter are staying with me. They went to Chalchuapa today, but they'll be back this afternoon."

"Where are the two little dogs?"

"The family took them along, because Laura can't live without them. Just imagine: since they didn't want them to travel in the baggage compartment, Laura's mother bought plane seats for them, just as if they were people. At first the airline didn't want to do it, but if you have money you can get away with anything."

Luisa was quiet while the two sisters chatted.

"Do all the toys have covers on them too?" she asked finally.

"No, not the toys," Lipa laughed. "Would you like to play with them for a while?"

Luisa shook her head.

"Come along, and I'll show you something you've probably never seen."

The servants' quarters were at the rear of the house. Lipa stopped before a green-painted door. She took an enormous bunch of keys from her apron pocket and sorted through them until she found the right one. The room smelled musty, and Lipa opened the windows. All the walls were covered with wooden wardrobes and long shelves.

"This is called the Ancestor Room," she said solemnly. "Hasn't Laura ever brought you here?"

"No." Luisa edged closer to Chabe.

"I have to air it out once a week," Lipa said as she opened the first wardrobe. It was filled with clothing, hats and shoes.

"In this closet," she announced proudly, "we keep the General's uniforms. This is the one he wore when he was inaugurated as president." She pointed out a uniform adorned with gold brocade.

"The threads are pure gold," she breathed.

"This is the dress the grandmother wore on the same occasion." She took out a dress of gray silk lace.

Luisa was amazed. Bit by bit she overcame her timidity and stroked the satin shoes, tried on a black

28

feathered hat and pulled a silver fox furpiece about her shoulders.

Lipa and Chabe were shaking with laughter.

"Don't you ever tell Laura," Lipa warned her. "For the family, these things are sacred. Would you like to see Niña Virginia's wedding dress?"

She opened the next wardrobe and took out a white dress embroidered with pearls.

"This is more work than any of the others," she sighed. "Heaven help me if it starts turning yellow. It's a good thing they're always bringing back new products from Europe and the United States. The veil served as mosquito netting for Laura when she was a baby." Lipa pointed to a crib that was lined with satin and adorned with embroidered ribbons.

Luisa was fascinated. They went through all the wardrobes. There were frock coats, evening gowns, top hats, broad-brimmed Italian straw hats. Luisa identified the dress Laura had worn for her First Communion three years earlier. Her grandmother, who was still alive then, had given her granddaughter a million dollars on that occasion. Laura's first baby shirt was also there. It was all embroidered and so fine it could have been stuffed in a walnut shell.

The shelves were filled with dolls: rows and rows of Italian Lenche dolls, Japanese dolls, porcelain dolls, the kind that have blue eyes and are always smiling. Naturally, they only saved the best ones and gave the others away.

"I think this is Niña Virginia's favorite room," Lipa said. "She's always explaining to me and to Niña Laura the significance of each article. She says that's called 'tradition.' It's as if she wished time would stand still. Poor Niña Virginia; she's very sentimental. And don't you tell Laura I brought you here; they might not like it. I'm the only one of the servants," she smiled proudly, "who is permitted to enter this room."

29

EROSION

I arose early
your memory
clouding my vision
I sought your face
in old and recent photos
and none was you
I read again the letters
that have lost the timbre
of your voice
and I bristled at your death
at your invented face
at my face I invent
at the skulking fear
of your death
at your life
(galloping death)
at all those daily deaths
that fall drop by drop
and erode my face.

TAKING THE VOWS

"Just think! In a few minutes we're going to see God."
Isabel gazed at Luisa with round eyes.

The two little girls, both dressed in white, were seated on a bench in the chapel. Each held a basket of white flowers and wore a circlet of jasmine about her head. They were maids of honor for Sor Ana Teresa, who would soon appear in her bridal gown to be married to God.

"Here she comes," Luisa squirmed around on the bench, "but she's all by herself."

Sor Ana Teresa paused for a moment, framed in the chapel doorway. She turned her head this way and that as if seeking someone and then began to walk slowly toward the altar. Father Agapito came forward to meet her and motioned to the two girls to draw closer. Sor Ana Teresa was pale. She looked about her again, her eyes shining with tears.

After the lengthy mass was over, four nuns pushed the benches to either side. The chapel was almost empty; only the closest members of the bride's family had been permitted to attend. The nuns spread a black sheet on the floor and placed enormous white candles at each corner. The mother superior approached the pew where Sor Ana Teresa knelt, removed her bridal veil, and with a huge pair of shears hacked off her lovely chestnut hair just above the ears.

Sor Ana Teresa arose and walked to the center of the chapel with her hands clasped and her gaze lowered. She stretched out on the spread sheet, and the nuns covered her, head and all, with another black sheet that had a silver cross embroidered in the center. The candles were lit, and Father Agapito announced that she had died to the world. He motioned to the two girls to scatter their flowers over her prostrate body.

31

Little by little, the people began to depart. Isabel and Luisa trembled silently. "Why didn't God show up?" Luisa asked herself. "If he had, I'll bet he wouldn't have let them cut off all that lovely hair."

THE VERSAILLES TENEMENT

"You don't know how lucky you are," Luisa told him, "to live in Versailles."

"If you say so," Memo shrugged.

The two of them were talking through one of the barred windows of Luisa's house.

Her maternal grandfather had studied in Paris when he was young, and every day after dinner he tried to revive his memories, describing to her in minute detail the monuments, the churches, the Parisian streets lined with chestnut trees and bustling outdoor cafes. What Luisa loved the most was the Versailles Palace with its bird-filled woods and its interminable hall of mirrors. Why didn't they ever let her visit it? Her grandfather told her that the two most beautiful cities in the world were Santa Ana and Paris, and she had an enormous desire to walk through the woods by the tenement across from her house. Why didn't her parents ever visit it? Not even her grandfather. Why didn't they ever let her go and play there?

One afternoon while she was sitting at the window telling herself stories, she saw her friend approaching. He carried something in his hands.

"Look," Memo was flustered, "I caught this pigeon in the woods." He thrust the trembling white bird through the bars into Luisa's hands.

"It's beautiful," she said.

"You keep it. I caught it for you."

"No," said Luisa, "she'd grow sad in a cage."

"I think she'd be fine here," Memo gazed down at his bare feet.

"My grandfather says that birds should be free," Luisa protested.

"It's just that..." Memo twisted his filthy toes in anguish, "my ma wants to kill her because we don't have anything to eat."

OPERATION HEROD

– for Jane

In my country
some time ago
the soldiers
began killing children
bruising the tender flesh
of children
tossing babies
into the air
on bayonets.
For each dead child
ten guerrillas are born
from each one
of these mutilated bodies
the virus of fury sprouts
it is dust
it is light
multiplying itself
the stifled tears of mothers
water it
and the Herods die
riddled by worms.

THE PRESIDENT'S SHEET

Before Paulina turned to prostitution, she started selling off everything her mother had left her. Her grandfather too had been a president of the republic, and she had inherited the porcelain dinner service with its initials and gold borders, the silverware, some jewelry and a linen sheet with his hand-embroidered monogram.

The only thing left was the sheet, and one fine day she decided the time had come to get rid of that. She went to the marketplace and, to the stupefaction of the market ladies and passersby, she opened it, helped by her younger sister who later became a nun, and began crying out:

"I'm selling the sheet of my grandfather, the president. He was the best president El Salvador ever had. Who will buy the sheet that so frequently caressed his body? This sheet has borne witness to his fatigues and his loves. It should be in a museum, but times are hard and I have to sell it."

Somebody went running to her rich aunt with the story, and before she found a client, a liveried chauffeur arrived in a navy blue limousine. He stuffed a crumpled bill into Paulina's hands and carried off the sheet.

THE NICARAGUAN
GREAT-GRANDFATHER (1)

– For Ritalejandra

"Your Nicaraguan great-grandfather, Tata Pedro, had a terrible temper," Don Serafín López told Luisa. "One day, for no particular reason, he went into a rage and started lashing about with his cane. One of the blows caught your grandfather in the eye and poked it out. I got to know Tata Pedro very well, even though I was much younger. He was one of the most capricious men, and one of the biggest landowners, in the Segovias. He lived in San Rafael where he was a prominent political leader. As might have been expected, he quarreled with the mayor and in another of his attacks of fury, he shouted:

"I'm leaving this sinkhole, and I'm taking everything with me." Sure enough, he rounded up a group of families and told them, "We're going to go and found another town, and you're going to help me tear down this house."

The house was made of adobe bricks. The people loaded them all into leather panniers and transported them on muleback to the new site. The wooden floors, the tile roof, the beams, the window frames: they hauled everything away. They even dug up the *guanabana* and orange trees plus a *cortés* and an oak tree and replanted them in the new location. My grandmother owned the new house after Tata Pedro died, and there are all those trees today with trunks this big all around the new house, which was almost identical to the old one. Tata Pedro had every single thing carried on the backs of mules or people from San Rafael del Norte clear to La Concordia. That's the name of the town your great-grandfather founded.

37

FIRST COMMUNION

Everything was ready for the party the night before. Chabela, Luisa's *nana*, had just finished ironing the pleated organdy dress that reached to the girl's ankles, and the wide, vaporous veil. Her mother gave the final touches to the table. It was covered with several damask tablecloths, and it extended the entire length of the patio corridor. The cake, surmounted by a tiny doll dressed just like Luisa, was going to occupy the very center.

"Off to bed now," Chabe told her, "and remember to drink a glass of water, because tomorrow morning you can't – not so much as a drop."

Luisa knew that even if she drank tons of water that night, she would wake up horribly thirsty, but there was no help for it. Her mother, Chabe, her aunts, had all told her it was to be the most important day of her life, and she had to make some sacrifice for it.

"Come along," Chabe told her, "let's get to bed."

Luisa followed her obediently.

When Chabe turned off the light, Luisa called her to her side.

"Is it true that tomorrow I can ask for anything I want and I'll get whatever I ask for?"

"That depends. You can ask for one thing – something that's very important to you.

"What should I ask for, Chabe?"

"How should I know? That God keeps your parents safe and sound for many years, that you remain pure and healthy and good. You're the one who has to decide."

Luisa lay for a long time with her eyes wide open in the darkness. The next morning, both Chabe and her mother helped her get dressed. She was dying of thirst, her new shoes pinched her feet and the cap that sustained her veil was terribly hot, but she didn't complain, not even once. What she was going to ask for was very important, and she had to make some sacrifice so it would be granted her.

Her father honked impatiently from the street, and Luisa went running out and climbed into the front seat so her dress wouldn't get wrinkled. Two nuns from Assumption College, dressed in heavy purple habits and cream-colored veils, were at the entrance to receive her, and they accompanied her into the chapel, which was already filled with schoolgirls. As Luisa entered, the choir up in the chapel loft started singing, and she felt her eyes filling with tears. The nuns escorted her to her prayer bench, which was covered with satin. Father Agapito, dressed in a white chasuble embroidered in gold thread and accompanied by a sacristan, gave the benediction and began to say mass.

Luisa opened her small, mother-of-pearl missal and followed the mass attentively. After a long time the nuns came for her and accompanied her to the altar. Luisa knelt, opened her mouth discreetly and received the host. With her head lowered and her hands clasped against her breast, she returned to her prayer pew, feeling slightly dizzy.

"It's now, right now that you have to make your wish," her internal voice told her.

"Dear Little Jesus," Luisa said under her breath, "I don't want to be married; I don't like the way men treat women, but I do want to have a baby, Dear Jesus, and Chabe says that only married women can have babies. So that's why I ask you with all my heart to let me get married, and as soon as I have my baby, to let my husband die."

The host dissolved in her mouth, and Luisa lifted her gaze, a beatific smile illuminating her features.

WHERE WAS YOUR CHILDHOOD LOST?

– For Daniel Frederick

From the framed corner
of the mirror
your photo watches me
it is your face
yet it isn't
behind it lurks your death
your unsuspected death
burning your eyes
thousands of dead children
and dead youths
and all of them are you
in you converge
your absence is more real
than your presence
they died tortured
died suddenly
died in jail
no one suspecting
it was his death
where was your childhood lost?
your luminous, truncated
adolescence?

THE NICARAGUAN
GREAT-GRANDFATHER (2)

Someone told Tata Pedro there was a treasure at the bottom of Hidden Lake.

From that day on, Tata Pedro knew no ease. He got it into his head that he would find the treasure, and he rounded up a gang of workers, armed with bars, picks and shovels.

"We have to open a ditch here," he told them. "We're going to drain this lake, and then we'll divide the treasure."

They all set to work with great enthusiasm, but about the fourth day, two of the ten workers who made up the gang said that they were quitting. Two days later another man left.

"What's going on?" Tata Pedro inquired indignantly. "How can anyone walk out on a simple job like this, and one that will be so well-paid?"

"It's not that," the oldest of them ventured. "It's because they've told us in the village that what we're doing is very dangerous."

"Why should it be dangerous?"

"They say the treasure was hidden by the Indians when the white man came, and they placed a curse on the lake. It seems there's a winged serpent guarding the treasure, and if we keep on draining the lake he's going to finish us all off."

"Old wives' tales!" Tata Pedro stormed. "How can grown men like you believe such things?"

"A good many people have seen him sticking his head out of the water, and if you want the truth, I'm leaving myself."

"Get lost with your whole gang of fairies!" Tata Pedro shouted, "and never let me lay eyes on you again."

Nobody showed up for work the following day, but Tata Pedro continued doggedly with his pick and shovel, more determined than ever that he was going to salvage the treasure.

RAINY DAY

Never again this rain
nor that stain of light
on the mountain crag
nor the border
of that cloud
nor your fleeting, immobile
smile
never again this instant
that already says goodbye
through your eyes.

AUNT FILIBERTA
AND HER CRETONNES

At least three times a year an ox-cart would stop in front of Luisa's house, and from it would descend Aunt Filiberta and all her children (she was always nursing the youngest), accompanied by innumerable junk-filled sacks and bundles of all shapes and sizes. There was no choice but to receive her. Amidst a flood of tears she would tell her sister that Alfonso had beaten her again, and she would install herself in the living room. She slept on the sofa with the baby, while the rest of the kids were scattered all over the house.

Luisa's father eyed her, horrified, and spent more time than usual playing billiards in the Casino.

Four or five nights later her husband would hire a serenade for her, and the following morning, with his pistol at his belt and his felt hat cocked over his left eyebrow, he would come around in his truck to pick her up. Luisa's mother would help her make up all the bundles once more. Aunt Filiberta would thank her, and with a smile that wavered between happiness and shame she would board the truck, followed by all her children, while the kids from the ghetto across the street surrounded the vehicle excitedly, and the Guards peered out from the barred windows of the fortress.

That same afternoon, Aunt Filiberta invariably would go running off to the Turk, Gadala María, where she'd buy yards and yards of flowered cretonne to change the curtains and re-cover all the furniture in the house.

44

FAREWELLS

"It's your siesta time"
I say with a stealthy glance
at the clock
"Yes"
you look at me with unfocussed eyes
I take your shoes off
remove your combs
cover you with the sheet
and kiss your forehead
the suitcases await me
only half-packed
I wedge in a book
a gift
bedroom slippers
Alberto backs the car out
hits the gas pedal
impatiently
half-stumbling
I go down the stairway
and stop at your door
should I open it
shouldn't I?
I peer through the crack
I have to see you again
one last time
I want to weep
watch over you
flee from you
cradle you in my arms.
Alone with Alberto
how can I tell him?

Last night
while we unwrapped tamales
and the air filled
with an odor of *lorocos*
I knew I couldn't go
without telling him
his boys were there
with their ready-made phrases
waiting to spit them out
and above all you
your forsakenness.
We tried to bridge the gap
with childhood memories
silences are brusque
the necessary phrase
forms on my lips
we've reached El Congo
by the old road
the one we used when young
the car stops at a bend
they are the same women
with their sales baskets
the same weary faces
the same dirty children
who draw near
the same uncontrollable sadness
how is it possible he doesn't see
all this heaped-up misery
doesn't hear the wailing
disguised in the hawker's cries
doesn't accept the message
of these eyes?
The car starts up again
you're asleep far away
with your death growing

Alberto lecturing me
to stop sowing hatred
with my writings
I with my ready phrase
refusing to spill out.

THE NICARAGUAN
GREAT-GRANDFATHER (3)

"Get that out of your head, Pedro," great-grandmother told him. "Be content with what we have; it's a sin to want more."

Great-grandfather frowned and didn't reply. The two finished eating in silence, and early the following morning he went off to continue digging.

After some days he suffered from insomnia. Great-grandmother listened to him tossing and turning in the bed. At daybreak he got up without saying a word.

That went on for more than a week. Tata Pedro grew thinner and thinner. The seat of his pants hung down to the back of his knees, and the purple bags under his eyes covered half of his face.

"It's God's punishment," great-grandmother mused without daring to tell him so directly, and she began to do the seven Mondays of the Lord of Mercy. On the fourth Monday, great-grandfather came home earlier than usual and scolded her for not watering the rosebush that was drying out. Great-grandmother paid no attention to him and went on darning his socks placidly.

"I'm getting tired of this nonsense," Tata Pedro said finally. "There's nothing up there: no serpent and no treasure."

"I'm happy for you, Pedro," she said without looking up from her darning. "You'll see that tonight you'll be able to sleep."

And that is just what happened, but then the headaches began. Every day at the same hour Tata Pedro felt his head was splitting. Great-grandmother stuffed him with aspirins, put fresh banana leaves on his forehead, gave him manzanilla tea. Nothing worked.

48

Finally they went to see the doctor in Estelí, and he couldn't do anything for Tata Pedro either.

"I say it's the serpent," great-grandmother told him. "You almost dried out its den, and now it's punishing you."

Tata Pedro glared at her and walked away without answering.

"Don't be so stubborn, Pedro," she called after him, "I know what I'm talking about. If you don't make another lake for the serpent, you'll never be cured."

Tata Pedro silently considered what his wife had told him, and every morning before noon, when his migraine punctually seized him, he wandered about the lake to see whether or not he might catch a glimpse of the serpent.

One day, almost by accident, his eyes fell upon the gully that had been the outlet of the almost-empty lake. He thought about it for a while, then began laughing out loud, and he set off to find the old man who had led the work gang.

"I discovered the treasure," he said.

"How's that? What do you mean?"

"There's a deep gully leading off from the lake, and we can build a dam across it to irrigate the whole valley. Understand what I'm saying? Let me show you before the headache hits me again."

The old man was enthused with Tata Pedro's discovery, and the following Monday – the seventh Monday great-grandmother had been observing – the original ten members of the work gang set about creating another lake, and Tata Pedro, magically, stopped suffering from headaches.

AT THE BEACH

That's nothing to cry over
come here
I'll tell you a story if you stop crying
the story happened in China.
Do you know where China is?
She shook her head
and reluctantly drew near
with her nose running
and her blue bathing trunks
clogged with sand.
A long time ago, I said
as I settled her on my lap,
far away in China
they bound women's feet
their bodies went on growing
only their feet
were imprisoned
beneath the bandages
and the poor women
could hardly walk
they had to let
their fingernails grow
until they were claws
rather than fingernails
and the poor women
could scarcely pick up a cup
to drink their tea.
It's not that they were useless
it's that their husbands
their fathers
their brothers
wanted them like that

a luxury object
or a slave.
This still happens
all around the world
it's not that their feet are bound
it's their minds, Ximena,
there are women who accept
and others who don't.
Let me tell you about
Rafaela Herrera:
with drums
and firecrackers
and flaming sheets
she frightened none other
than Lord Nelson.
Lord Nelson was afraid
he thought the whole town
had risen up
(he came from England to invade
          Nicaragua)
and returned home
defeated.
Your twisted thumb
is like being a woman
you have to use it a lot
and you'll see how well it heals.
Run along now and play
don't carry sand for the others
help your cousins
to build the castle
put towers on it
and walls
and terraces
and knock it down
and rebuild it
and keep on opening doors.

Don't carry sand
let them do it
for a while
let them bring you
buckets full of sand.

THE MYTH-MAKING UNCLES (1)

In Luisa's family there were many fabulous liars, including herself, of course. There was one very intelligent uncle who taught philosophy in the university. He was self-educated, but according to Wilf he possessed a culture that many European professors would have envied. He learned Greek by himself in order to read Plato in the original, and he also knew Latin.

After the massacre of 1932 he had to flee the country. He spent two years in Mexico, but he assured everybody that he had toured South America and that all alone, without a guide, he had crossed the Cordillera of the Andes on muleback.

Luisa was the only one who took him seriously. She would listen to him, fascinated, and her uncle, growing more and more excited, would add new adventures to his repertoire.

On his return from Mexico, he was asked to give a lecture. He spoke on Henri Bergson and told how they had met at the Sorbonne and became fast friends. He recounted many amusing anecdotes about the eminent philosopher and related a trip the two of them had made to the south of France.

He was so convincing that many friends who had known him since his youth and who knew perfectly well that, apart from his single trip to Mexico, he had spent his entire life in Santa Ana, surrounded by books and atlases, began to doubt their own memories. The French consul was enthused and came up to him after the lecture to congratulate him. He said that he also had studied at the Sorbonne, and the two of them spent the rest of the night drinking beer and reminiscing about Paris.

53

NOT YET

> "And how can we sing with a
> foreign foot over our heart?"
>
> – S. Quasimodo

Not yet
I can't go back yet
I am still forbidden
to plunge into your roads
to yield to your rivers
to contemplate your volcanos
to rest in the shade
of my *ceiba*.
From abroad I see you
my heart watches you
from abroad,
constricted, watches you
in memories
between wavering bars
of memory
that widen
and close
ebb and flow in my tears.
It is difficult to sing you
from exile
difficult to celebrate
your nebulous
jagged map.
I can't do it yet
a dry sob
sticks in my throat.
It is difficult to sing you

when a heavy boot
with foreign hobnails
tears and cleaves
your flesh.

RENE

Luisa was five years old when she first visited Nicaragua. Her cousin René, who was blonde, black-eyed and fair-skinned, and with whom she fell in love immediately, had just turned seven. René loved to talk about death. Luisa listened to him, fascinated, without understanding a thing he was saying. They became close friends within a few days, and to prevent their other cousins from interrupting their long metaphysical conversations, they would go and hide in the granary.

When René started in on his monologue about death, his voice changed completely; his tone became more grave, far different than when he took her on muleback down to the river and she would cling to his waist while the mule drank. Once he climbed down and left her there, wailing and helpless, until Manuel, his father, came running to her rescue.

Luisa preferred the other René: the one with the Sybilline voice, who spoke to her of death and told her that only she knew his secret. Manuel also knew it. Sometimes when he had drunk too much he would take off his belt and threaten to whip the boy unless he talked about death before Manuel's friends.

When Luisa returned to Santa Ana, Papa Lico gave her an enormous doll with black eyes and blonde hair, which she baptized René. A year went by, during which Luisa and her cousin never wrote each other. One morning the mailman delivered the little girl the first telegram she had ever received.

"It's for you," he told her. "It comes from Estelí."

Luisa opened it with trembling hands. It read bluntly: "René died last night." It was signed, "Manuel."

That same night she tore the doll's eyes out, and ever after that she could never open a telegram without her hands trembling uncontrollably.

TIME OF LOVE

When you love me
I drop my polished mask
my smile becomes my own
the moon becomes the moon
and these very trees
of this instant
the sky
the light
presences that open
into vertigo
and are newly born
and are eternal
and your eyes as well
are born with them
your lips that in naming
discover me.
When I love you
I am sure I don't end here
and that life is transitory
and death a transit
and time a blazing carbuncle
with no worn-out yesterdays
with no future.

MARGARITA'S BIRTHDAY

Margarita was a poor girl of humble extraction – a *mengala*, as they say in Santa Ana – but she was educated at the Assumption convent school because her parents wanted her to have "good" friendships.

When she turned 15 they gave a party for her. Her father scraped together the money to buy a ring set with a tiny diamond and hire a marimba, and everybody danced until 10 p.m.

Margarita's godmother was one of the richest ladies in Santa Ana, and of course they invited her. Margarita was certain that she would present her with a beautiful gift – perhaps a jewel or a dress from abroad. A girl's 15th birthday is an important occasion, and a godmother has certain obligations.

Finally, after keeping everyone waiting, Doña Celia arrived with a large package wrapped in colored paper. Margarita's parents outdid themselves in attending her, offering her a glass of Spanish sherry and hors d'oeuvres of chicken paté. Margarita came running, beautiful in her new sky-blue dress. She kissed her godmother, took the package from her and went off to her room, followed by her curious friends.

"Hurry up!" they coaxed her while Margarita unwrapped the package slowly in order to enhance the surprise.

Finally the gift was disclosed. It was a tin of cookies. Margarita's face fell in disappointment. "What a drag!" she looked up at her friends. But it was a nice box with colorful flowers stamped against a blue background. Margarita pried it open to offer cookies to her friends. But the box was empty, except for a few stale crumbs clinging to the corners.

ARE YOU MEMORY?

I don't know if with your death
you have stayed behind
– are you memory? –
or have taken a sudden
                         leap
that I must tread
to catch up with you.

FELIX

Felix was lovely. Skinny and lovely, with big sad eyes. He was more or less Luisa's age: about eight years old. After the massacre of 1932 her father had found the boy wandering about. They had killed his parents, his two smaller brothers and his grandmother. His only remaining relative was an uncle who was in jail for murder.

Luisa was happy when he arrived. Since he was full of lice they had to shave his head, and the next day they bought him pants, shirts and shoes. He didn't like the shoes. He finally accepted a pair of sandals, but he'd always take them off whenever he could.

Felix slept in a small room next to the back patio. He started school and in less than two months he learned to read.

"The boy is intelligent," Luisa's father was happy. "After he gets through primary school, we'll have to see he learns a trade."

One afternoon when the girl's parents were out, she, Felix and Beto, her younger brother, were playing ball, and Felix accidentally broke one of the colored glass panes in the screen that separated the living quarters from her father's office.

"Just wait, you little bastard," Dalila told him. She didn't like Felix because she was some kind of Evangelist, and every time the Holy Spirit possessed her and she got the shakes, Felix would nearly die laughing. "The Doctor is going to give you a walloping like you never had."

Luisa and Beto tried to soothe him, telling him that they were all to blame and they would say so; that if he got a beating, they'd have to get one too, and that Dalila was fibbing, because their father was really very good.

61

There was nothing to be done. The maid's threat was too much, and Felix ran away, taking only what he wore on his back. He even left his sandals behind.

Luisa's father was furious when he learned about it. He fired Dalila on the spot, and the next day he went to Juayúa to speak to the mayor to see if the latter could locate him. He put advertisements in the newspapers with a photograph of Felix that he himself had taken, and he told the Guards to be on the lookout for him when they went patrolling, and if they brought him home, he'd give them a reward. It was all in vain. Days, months and years went by, and Felix never reappeared.

DISILLUSIONMENT

I machinegunned tourists
for the liberation
of Palestine.
I massacred Protestants
for the independence of Ireland.
I poisoned aborigines
in the Amazon jungles
to open the way
for urbanization
and progress.
I assassinated Sandino
Jesus
and Martí.
I exterminated Mai-Lai
in the name of democracy.
Nothing has done any good:
despite my efforts
the world goes on the same.

Luisa grew nostalgic during the trip to Estelí. She recalled the granary filled with ears of corn where she and René had gone to hide from their other cousins. She remembered the well, the araucaria tree, the excursions on muleback to the river. It was summertime, and everything was dusty. They left the car next to the gasoline station, had lunch in a small neighborhood restaurant and began hunting for the house. They had been in Estelí two years before, but it was difficult to find. The huge araucaria, its bottom branches blackened by fire, was nowhere visible.

"I'm sure it's around here," Bud said, trying to recognize the three blue walls that had remained standing.

"Excuse me," Luisa addressed a woman who was passing by, "could you tell me how to find the house where the Solórzano sisters lived?"

"Who are you?"

"Luisa Solórzano, the daughter of Dr. Guillermo Solórzano."

"From El Salvador?" the woman fluttered.

"Yes," Luisa replied.

"Come along with me."

She began shouting, "Doña Adela, Doña Adela," as they entered a dark passageway. A tall, bony old lady in her seventies materialized, followed by a boy who shrank timidly against the wall. Luisa turned to give Bud a terrified glance.

"This is the Doctor's daughter," the woman said.

"You must be Luisa," Doña Adela said. She was a ghostly presence in the darkness. "Come this way," she gestured as the other woman left them.

They entered a living room that was also murky.

"Go call Miguel," Doña Adela ordered the boy without turning to look at him, "and tell María to bring some ice cream."

"Please don't bother," Luisa said, dreading an interminable visit, "we have to be back in Managua before five."

"It's barely two," Doña Adela said impassively as she pulled the curtains open. There was a pervasive musty odor. Obviously, they never opened the room unless they had visitors.

"What brings you here?" the old lady asked.

"A whim of my daughter's," Luisa smiled uncomfortably. "She just had a baby girl, and she wants us to bury the umbilical cord in the lot where my father's house stood."

Doña Adela was silent for a while.

"My daughter-in-law owns an ice cream shop," she said finally.

After about ten minutes that seemed to Luisa like hours, María appeared with her hair in curlers and a tray of ice cream. Behind her clumped a corpulent man wearing boots.

"My children, Miguel and María," Doña Adela announced without altering her tone of voice or her expression. The boy reappeared and scuttled over to stand behind Doña Adela's chair.

María distributed the ice creams and sat down beside her husband on the red plastic sofa. The boy (Luisa noticed for the first time) had the lax features of the mentally retarded. After a few desultory sentences, Doña Adela disappeared with the boy behind her. The conversation with Miguel and María was an uphill struggle. Bud glanced despairingly at his wristwatch. Finally Doña Adela reappeared.

"Everything is ready," she announced as she headed toward her wicker chair, trailed by her young shadow.

65

"Those are Miguel's sons," she indicated with a glance two robust adolescents who nodded at them from the doorway.

"Shall we go now?" Luisa ventured.

"When you finish your ice cream," the old lady decreed.

Bud and Luisa hastened to empty their ice cream cups.

"Follow me," Doña Adela said as she rose from her chair. "The next-door neighbor bought the lot and has a vegetable stand there now."

"No wonder I didn't recognize the place," Bud murmured. "They cut down the araucaria."

Doña Adela repeated the story of the umbilical cord to the new owner, who gazed at them in astonishment and motioned them to pass through. Following the firm footsteps of the old lady, the delegation threaded its way in Indian file among heaps of *huisquiles*, carrots, tomatoes and Italian squash. It was only then that Bud and Luisa became aware that the two adolescents behind them were armed with a pick and shovel.

"I think it should be right here by the wall," Doña Adela addressed her grandsons.

"There's no need for a big hole," Bud drew a jackknife from his pocket. "I can open it with this."

"No," Doña Adela said in the same flat tone, "the pigs will eat it."

Four small black pigs turned to look at them with curiosity.

"A daughter of mine is buried here," the old lady commented as her grandsons opened the hole and the subnormal boy stared at Luisa and Bud with his mouth half-open. "She died on me when she was very small."

The delegation fell silent, all eyes fixed on the hole.

"I think it's all right," Bud ventured.

"A little deeper," Doña Adela ordered.

When the hole was finally to the old lady's liking, Luisa deposited the umbilical cord, wrapped in gauze, in the bottom, and the boys refilled the hole and tamped down the earth.

They returned in Indian file again amid the heaps of vegetables, thanked the vegetable lady, who inspected Luisa and Bud as if they were from some other planet, and when they reached the sidewalk, despite Doña Adela's flat-voiced entreaty that they go back inside for a while, Bud and Luisa began saying goodbye.

"Next time you come by, bring me some perfume from Europe," Doña Adela told Luisa by way of farewell.

The boy, ever close by her side, started hopping up and down and, squeezing her arm tightly, he whimpered: "Mama, mama, you haven't even introduced me to them."

EPITAPH

I don't want a gravestone
over my body
only fresh grass
and a flowering jasmine.

CIPITIO

Mama Nela knew many things: she played "The Blue Danube" on the piano, made tiny animals out of bread crumbs, dressed fleas, made the most beautiful piñatas in Santa Ana, and above all, she knew how to tell stories. It was she who told Luisa, while pulling threads out of a multi-colored bundle for the quilt she was sewing, how the Siguanaba bewitched men and left them idiotized, and about the white *cadejo* and the other, the black one, that everybody said was bad, but to whom she was very grateful because whenever her husband or one of her sons went on a bender, he was the one who protected them.

The character Luisa liked best was Cipitío.

"He's a scrawny little dwarf," Mama Nela laughed, "who keeps his hair slicked down with vaseline. He wears a hat with an enormously wide brim, and when he likes a girl, he strews flower petals along the path where she is going to pass and conceals himself in a doorway or behind a tree to recite verses for her."

Luisa listened to her, fascinated. One of her greatest desires was that, when she was a bit more grown up, Cipitío, who according to Mama Nela was even more amorous than Uncle Alfonso, would notice her and carpet her path with *maquilishuat* flowers.

69

EACH TIME

Each time I love you
life and death
are present:
daybreak
and nightfall
paradise
sepulcher.

JAMIE IN PONELOYA

"Tell me about Jamie," Luisa said to Milán, who had just returned from Nicaragua.

"He's a real revolutionary," Milán grinned. "Even though he's not old enough, he joined the militia as a mascot. He trains with them twice a week, does his best on the obstacle course, knows how to fieldstrip a BZ, goes on long marches carrying his rifle and sleeps with his boots on like the rest."

"Incredible!" Luisa felt her eyes moisten, "he's such a little kid, barely ten years old."

"Two weeks ago," Milán continued, "I took him with me to Poneloya. We stayed in that old weatherbeaten hotel that faces the sea. It must have been built at the turn of the century. The partitions between the rooms don't reach the ceiling, and you can hear everything that's going on in the other rooms.

Before going to sleep, Jamie always sings the Sandinista hymn. When I turned out the light, he said goodnight to me and began singing. A little girl in the next room joined in on the second verse, and I began humming along so he wouldn't feel embarrassed. Next, the little girl's parents started singing, then a boy down the hall, and the music kept swelling until at the end, everyone in the hotel filled with internationalists and *nicas*, was accompanying him from the darkness of their rooms."

MY CITY

"The city must always
be following you."

– C. P. Cavafy

I dreamt that my city
was following me
I heard the internal music
of its insects
its foliage
its rock-strewn river
its odor obsessed me
its vaporous aromas
and sour sweatiness
and I wanted to flee from my city
from its muted groans
and rancid odors
and it followed me
with its row of faces
and streets
and its veiled laughter
and I wanted to reprimand it
and it turned invisible
with no lights
or shadows
and its absence pained me
and nostalgia flowered in my dreams:
I retraced childhood paths
dreamt of friends I lost
of the trees
and the leaves I lost
of the town-hall band
of the *chiltota* nests

72

MALINCHE

This morning
in the mail
a child's drawing:
black trees
withered branches
heads dangling
like seedpods.
"A refugee child,"
Rosa says in her letter
the skull facing me
is winking one eye.
The child knows it all
guesses it
five hundred years ago
Malinche
handed the invader
her continent
handed it over out of love
out of madness.
He always knew it
knew it yesterday
when he watched
his father's head fall
while trying
to tell him something.
Treacherous Malinche
the blossoms of her love
dropped away
and there remained heads
dangling like seedpods.
Fifty years ago
the bewitched tree

(the Indian girl repented
and embraced it weeping)
again produced
a harvest of skulls
Izalco wept
dry tears
and the country mourned.
The most recent harvest
has been the richest:
children
girls
men
the people's red blood
exploding in the air.
The malinche tree is perfidious
the Indian girl baptized it
bewitched it.
The child knows it all
he senses it
his last glimpse
as he flees:
the doors and windows
half-open
the marauding soldiers
among the black trees.
He always knew it
ever since yesterday
drops of blood
are the fallen petals
and from the branches
dangle heads
like seedpods.

THE GYPSY (1)

"You're stupid," the Gypsy told Luisa. "You'll never know what it cost me to convince Cipitío to bring you a serenade. He said it wasn't worth it, because you were scarcely fourteen and a bourgeois to boot, and on top of all that he'd never so much as laid eyes on you. I lied to him and told him you were really a cute kid and a lot of stuff like that. Finally, through sheer flirtatiousness, I got him to come along, and there you were, snoring your head off."

"When was this?"

"Last night, about 11 o'clock. He had another engagement before midnight."

"Did he like the cross?"

"I don't think he even looked at it. I've never heard him so inspired. He sang *rancheras*, *boleros*, tangos, and accompanied himself on the guitar. If you'd only stuck your head out the window, right now you'd have your sidewalk carpeted with flower petals. After half an hour of whanging away on his guitar he said, 'You see? I told you it wasn't worth it. These teeny-boppers are all a bunch of brats.' He took an enormous swig of *chicha*, crammed a banana into his mouth and off he went.

LUISA'S PAINTINGS

Luisa always wanted to be a painter, but she had no talent. For her, painting was magic. She frequented museums and went to all the exhibits she could, because she was certain that in one of the pictures she would discover the secret: suddenly, right there in the center of the painting a door would open to let her into that other reality, which until now she had only conjectured.

Luisa imagined pictures that she was never able to transfer to the canvas, but one night she began to paint in her dreams. At the outset she used huge canvases of two by three meters with horizontal swatches of red shading into orange, or of violets that faded into white. Sometimes it took her several nights to finish a painting. She would think about it during the day, seeking solutions, and she would go to bed as early as possible in order to get back to work

She spent a long time – more than a year – painting. The pictures grew smaller but were much more detailed. She painted artichokes; cabbages with eyes, noses or ears lurking in the leaves; trains filled with people that climbed and swooped down roller coaster mountains; plazas filled with empty chairs; black-frocked pastors preaching to starving dogs and two-legged cows.

Luisa began to think of organizing an exhibit. She had at least 70 canvases. The problem was finding a gallery. She would invite a group of her friends from that side to the opening: those she kept meeting in that other dimension.

One night she suddenly stopped painting. At first she gave the matter no importance; she must simply be tired and in need of a vacation. The terrible thing was that she had stopped painting when she was half-finished with a picture that disturbed her a great deal. She had gone back

78

to swatches of colors. This one was a large canvas in different shades of gray with a line of red dots crossing it. The line went off the canvas on one side, and Luisa spent many days wondering how to finish it. She didn't know what the red dots signified. They didn't really fit into the painting and she wanted to eliminate them: the line of red dots that began dripping and running just before they went off the canvas.

A month went by, then two months. Luisa travelled to Nicaragua and began to work on something else, leaving behind that unfinished painting and the others – more than 70 of them – all stacked together.

I ALSO LIKE THAT LOVE

- To Sara Jennifer

I also like the love
that finds the door slammed shut
the one that enters through the window
pirouetting on a tightrope.

THE GYPSY (2)

That mad creature has found another impossible love, Luisa laughed to herself. I'll never really understand her. Despite her love of adventure, her wildness, her Utopian streak and the happiness bubbling up inside her, it is sadness that always leaves its mark on her face.

PREMATURE NECROLOGY

Mario's case was strange. The newspapers were constantly writing him off as dead, and just as constantly he would reappear with a broad smile, or he'd send Luisa a postcard from some weird place announcing a forthcoming visit. The third time this happened, Luisa smiled at the announcement, remembering her aunt Lola, who read the obituary column in the newspaper every day to learn whether or not she were still alive.

The Argentine Triple A condemned Mario to death, and the Buenos Aires newspapers announced his disappearance. Less than two weeks later, Luisa received a card with a photograph of one of those beautiful pre-Columbian vases on the front, telling her that he was in Lima and working like crazy. A few months later, Bud read a news item in *Le Monde*, reporting that Mario had been arrested in Lima and deposited on the Andean side of the border of Ecuador without suitcases. An Ecuadorean friend telephoned agitatedly to say that his government had deported Mario back to Buenos Aires.

Worse than a pingpong ball, Luisa thought, and she wept for him and began rereading his complete works and reminiscing with Bud about the lovely times they had spent together. In Buenos Aires at that time they were "disappearing" anybody who caused them the slightest bother, but Mario was lucky. Fifteen days later he surfaced again in Cuba and sent Luisa a postcard from the island with a note that read: "I've finally landed on *Terra Firma*."

DON'T THINK OF TOMORROW

Don't think of tomorrow
or make me promises
you won't be the same
nor will I be present.
Let's live together the crest of this love
with no deceits
no fears
transparent.

THE DEAF MUTES OF CA'N BLAU

The old stone house in Deyá in which Luisa and Bud lived was previously owned by an old lady who was a deaf mute and who hobbled about with the aid of a cane. She had already died when Luisa and Bud bought the house, and it was Uncle Juan, her brother, who closed the sale.

"She was very intelligent in spite of being a deaf mute," he told them. "She could communicate with everybody in town, and she'd make them laugh with her dramatic gestures. She was born right here in this room, and after she had a fall about twenty years ago she had to use this cane," he struck the floor with a gnarled olive branch. "I made it for her myself. It always accompanied her," he addressed Luisa, "and I'd like it to remain in this house." Luisa assured him she would take care of it, and she put it away in the back of the closet.

From time to time the old lady would materialize in Ca'n Blau. On several occasions Luisa caught a glimpse of her out of the corner of her eye. She would skim like a fleeting shadow through the living room and disappear into the kitchen. Luisa, of course, never mentioned these occasions to anybody; strange things were always happening to her, and she didn't want people to think she was crazy.

One evening, about 7, she was talking to some friends in the Ca'n Blau living room when Luisa saw Friedly's face turn pale. John jumped from his chair and asked:

"Did you see it too?"

"See what?" she asked, because this time she hadn't sensed anything.

"The figure of a small woman," John said. "She moved like a streak."

"She had a cane," Friedly added, "and she went into the kitchen."

They both got up to investigate, but of course they found nothing.

Years later, during one of Luisa and Bud's trips to Central America, they left Ca'n Blau in the hands of a woman rental agent while they were gone.

They received a letter from Elena Coll, the agent, one morning in Managua, informing them that she had rented the house to six charming dwarves. They had fallen in love with the house at first sight and had promised to take good care of it. All six were deaf mutes; they worked in a circus and had come to Deyá to spend their vacations.

TIME IS OBSTINATE

Time is obstinate
in its ebb and flow
and sculpts your face
and transforms you
and etches new marks
in my face.
Every night
with an oblique gesture
it repeats its hateful litany
and convokes my dead
and shows me your skull
and I dream tears
and the world dissolves
and slips through my fingers.

THE FLOOD

The flood left its mark on Santa Ana. It had rained torrentially for three days and three nights, and the river had overflowed. A broad current swept through the street in front of Luisa's house, bearing tree trunks, dead dogs and alley cats and occasionally a cow. It carried off a neighboring albino boy who ventured out of his house.

It was a terrible flood, and to make matters worse Luisa's father had gone off to Panama for an eye operation. The water flooded the corridors of the house and filled the patio. It was a muddy, brawling, tumultous current, more agitated than a river, and it swept away the tin and cardboard shacks of the poor. Many children died during those days, and it lasted for a week. Only Chabe, who was very brave, dared leave the house to buy the bare necessities of life at Niña Fina's store just around the corner. She went barefoot and moved very carefully, supporting herself against the walls of the neighboring houses.

The small boys of the Versailles *mesón* improvised rafts out of boards, and they offered to do people's shopping for them. One day the flood swept a dead pig down the street. They seized it excitedly, turning the raft over so they nearly drowned, but they managed to catch hold of the branch of a breadfruit tree beside the Guardia fortress and hauled the pig up into the tree with them. That night everyone had a banquet at the *mesón*.

THE RIVERS

The terrain in my country
is abrupt
the gullies go dry
in the summertime
and are stained with red
in the winter.
The Sumpul is boiling with corpses
a mother said
the Goascarán
the Lempa
are all boiling with the dead.
The rivers no longer sing
they lament
they sweep their dead along
cradle them
they twinkle
under the tepid moon
under the dark
accomplice night
they cradle their dead
the wounded
those who are fleeing
those who pass by
they grow irate
bubbling and seething
dawn draws near
almost within reach
the rivers are coffins
crystalline flasks
cradling their dead
escorting them
between their wide banks

the dead sail down
and the sea receives them
and they revive.

SUNDAY SIESTAS

"What's wrong, Paulina? Why don't you want to?"

"Don't feel like it," she blew another bubblegum globe and popped it. "There are too many people around."

There were six or seven kids bathing in the reservoir of the coffee mill that belonged to Ernesto's father. There were Paulina and Ricardito, her younger brother; Luisa and Beto; the two Gutiérrez boys and, of course, Ernesto, who was Paulina's cousin. Their parents had stayed talking on the shady veranda of the house. It was 3 in the afternoon, and the sun was baking hot.

"If you do it, I'll give you my old transistor radio," Ernesto offered.

"Do what?" Luisa asked.

"It's a new game that Paulina and Ricardito have learned," Ernesto explained, feeling the self-important host.

"Really and truly?" Paulina stood up, brushing the dirt off her wet bathing suit. "Okay, but on one condition. One of you is going to have to take his bathing suit off in front of everybody else, and I will choose who it will be."

She looked around at all the boys and and giggled as she pointed to Beto, who was barely eight years old.

"You," she said.

"Me?" Beto looked at her beseechingly. He was very timid in those days, and Paulina loved to tease him.

"You. If not, I won't play."

"What difference does it make, Beto? It's nothing," Ernesto encouraged him. "You'll see how interesting it is."

Beto looked at Luisa, imploring her support, but she only nodded yes. She was curious to watch the game.

Beto got up reluctantly and went around to the opposite corner of the water tank. He turned his back on them and reticently removed his trunks.

"Turn around," Paulina yelled.

Beto turned around slowly, covering himself with his trunks.

"Take your hand away," Paulina ordered.

For a second, or maybe a second and a half, he removed his hand, and everybody could see his wienie. It didn't matter to Luisa; she saw it every morning when they bathed together.

Paulina shrugged disdainfully.

"Ready, Ricardo?" she addressed her brother.

"I don't wanna."

"Don't be stupid. I'll let you listen to 'The Lone Ranger' every afternoon."

She stripped off her bathing suit impassively, spread it on the ground and lay down on it face up.

"Hurry up," she said impatiently.

Ricardito puffed out his cheeks and took off his trunks. As if by magic, his wienie straightened up and got hard. The other boys looked at each other in astonishment. He lay down on top of Paulina, and she helped guide it into place.

"Go ahead," she said, "don't act like a jerk."

He began moving his hips up and down.

"Tell us how you learned," Ernesto said in his master of ceremonies voice.

Paulina left off chewing her gum and turned to look at them innocently.

"My folks always take a long siesta on Sunday afternoons," she said, "and I'd hear strange noises in the bedroom. One time I hid in the closet and left the door a bit ajar. They were doing this, and they seemed to like it so much that I taught Ricardito how. You ought to try it; it's really easy."

THE MAD WOMAN OF
THE GRAND ARMEE

Luisa always felt a vague nostalgia each time she saw the prostitute of the Grande Armée preaching to the automobiles waiting for the traffic light to change before they turned into the circle of the Arch of Triumph. She was only amiable to green Peugeots; they were the only ones she would climb into. All other makes of cars were targets for her heated anathemas and profound contempt.

Luisa never understood her nostalgia until one night when she was returning from the movies with Bud, she suddenly remembered Crazy Pastora, wild-eyed and brandishing her cane as she harangued against social injustice on the dusty street corners of Santa Ana.

THERE'S ALWAYS
AN INTRUDER

There's always an intruder
in matters of love:
sometimes a glance
a torpid gesture
a phrase
an odor
a kiss that while joining
separates us.

ROQUE'S VIA CRUCIS

"You can see death reflected in that boy's face," Aurora told Luisa, referring to Roque Dalton.

"Nonsense!" Luisa exclaimed. "He has as many lives as a cat. He's always escaping death by the skin of his teeth. The first time he was saved by an earthquake. He was in the prison of Cojutepeque when an earthquake brought down a wall and he was able to wriggle out. The second time, he was only two days away from a firing squad when a *coup d'etat* overthrew Lemus, who was the dictator at that moment.

Roque and Luisa never knew each other personally, but they corresponded between Prague and Paris and delighted in writing each other about Salvadoran *pupusas*, rooster in *chicha*, bread with *chumpe*, and all the other exquisite flavors and aromas that were unavailable to them in Europe.

Once Luisa travelled to Cuba where Roque was awaiting her in the airport with a bunch of flowers, but her plane was delayed two days, and he had to travel to the interior of the island. From there he would send her notes, which were invariably delivered at lunchtime.

They never so much as embraced each other, but a mutual friend assured her that, according to Roque, Luisa taught him to dance the rumba.

Years later, that same friend called Luisa to announce Roque's death. The news was confused, imprecise and nobody yet knew who had assassinated him.

Luisa was deeply touched, and that same evening, in order to feel a bit closer to him, she had the urge to read aloud some of his poems. She opened his book at random, and the first verses her eyes encountered were:

"When you learn I have died,
don't pronounce my name."

SEEDS OF LIBERTY

They wanted to flatten El Salvador.
With heavy bulldozers
they ripped through your hills
steamrolled your soil
tore into a crust
of your history.
Strange plants
started sprouting
from the rocks they sprouted
from the cut banks
of the highway.
Someone spread the alarm
called in biologists
the regime's academicians
and foreign observers.
Since the Jurassic age
they affirmed
these types of plants
have never been seen
in the country.
This one is called Liberty
said the oldest wise man
this other one Justice
and that one over there
is Conscience.
The bulldozer returned
to uproot them.
The plants grew stronger
the guerrillas began
to flourish
the plants spread
along with the combats

the *muchachos* cover their heads
with the widest
most lustrous leaves:
long columns of ants
advancing toward the sun.
Airplanes don't see them
can't detect them
the bulldozers keep on
crushing rocks
opening highways
the seeds
were awaiting their chance
for milennia
the plants proliferated,
the guerrillas
more advisers
arrive
to consult with each other.
The *muchachos*
the plants
climb toward the future
toward the sun.

THE MYTH-MAKING UNCLES (2)

Another of Luisa's myth-making uncles was an unconditional admirer of the United States. He had studied at a military academy and made a hobby of buying medals and decorations at pawnshops, which he wore on his khaki field jacket. He claimed to have been a colonel in the U.S. army during the Second World War and to have won medals fighting against the Germans. The fact is, he was never in Europe, because the place simply didn't interest him. He spent the entire war living in the mansion that he had built on one of his coffee plantations, where he frequently entertained the U.S. ambassador and any Yankee who happened to be passing through El Salvador.

He thought gringo doctors were marvellous. He was riding a motorcycle one day, or so he claimed, when he collided with an army truck, and his right leg was totally severed. He picked it up from the ground, got back on his motorcycle and, despite his weakness and loss of blood, made it to the nearest field hospital. There, in less than an hour, they sewed his leg back on, and now it was just as good as the other one.

FARABUNDO MARTI

"Didn't Farabundo Martí enter this house about 20 minutes ago?" Colonel Salinas asked Luisa's father.

"No," he replied. "I've known Farabundo ever since we were at the University together. The only person who has knocked on the door in the past half hour was a beggar."

"Precisely. We have information that he has disguised himself as a beggar."

"Don't worry, Colonel," Luisa's father laughed, "I'd have recognized him."

"I'll take your word, Doctor, that you are telling me the truth," the Colonel said as he went out the door.

Farabundo, in fact, was hiding in her father's clinic. General Martínez, who was defense minister at the time, had issued an order for his arrest.

Luisa's father went out to make his routine visits to his patients so as not to attract the attention of the Guards across the street. The only one with whom he shared the secret was Luisa's mother, who took some sweet rolls and coffee to the fugitive and remained conversing with him for a while. About 6 in the afternoon, Luisa's father returned home and sat down to read the newspaper as usual, so as not to arouse suspicions among the servants. Half and hour later, he slipped Farabundo into the garage, helped him into the trunk, and drove him to the Guatemalan border.

NIGHTMARE IN CHINANDEGA

"When we took the fortress of Chinandega," Carlos told Luisa one day in San Juan del Sur, "one of the *compas* came to tell us he heard moaning at the bottom of a well. We investigated and, sure enough, there amidst the bodies of twenty *compas* that were already crawling with worms, we discovered a pregnant woman who had lost her mind.

"We pulled her out, screaming and covered with worms. She couldn't tell us anything, but we knew she had been thrown into the well on orders of the commandant.

"We confronted him with the facts, and he tried to deny them. The bastard was trembling. He was one of Somoza's most savage torturers. I told him that the people would judge him, and we took him out to the main plaza. You should have seen what that was like; they nearly lynched him. We had to execute him right there on the spot.

"We sent the woman to a hospital, and she died two days later without recovering her sanity."

BECAUSE I WANT PEACE

Because I want peace
and not war
because I don't want to see
hungry children
squalid women
men whose tongues
are silenced
I have to keep on fighting.
Because there are clandestine
cemeteries
and Squadrons of Death
drug-crazed killers
who torture
who maim
who assassinate
I want to keep on fighting.
Because on the peak
of Guazapa
my brothers peer out
from their bunkers
at three battalions
trained in Carolina
and Georgia
I have to keep on fighting.
Because from Huey helicopters
expert pilots
wipe out villages
with napalm
poison the rivers
and burn the crops
that feed the people
I want to keep on fighting.

Because there are liberated zones
where people
learn how to read
and the sick are cured
and the fruits of the soil
belong to all
I have to keep on fighting.
Because I want peace
and not war.

GRANNY AND THE GOLDEN BRIDGE

Manuel had an endless store of anecdotes about his crazy grandmother who owned a small hut on a strip of ground half a kilometer from the Golden Bridge.

"She was crazy, but a very active old lady," he grinned reminiscently, "and terribly proud of her huge bridge spanning the Lempa River. 'My little bridge,' she used to call it."

Everybody else in El Salvador called it the "Golden Bridge," because with contractors' kickbacks to high government officials and inflated materials and labor estimates, it had cost the Salvadoran taxpayers three or four times as much as it should have.

Manuel was the leader of the Salvadoran peasant organization, who had been invited to Europe on a speaking tour.

"Why do you say she was crazy?" Luisa asked.

"After the civil war started, the army stationed troop units at either end of the bridge to protect it and to control traffic crossing it. It occurred to Granny that she could make her fortune by cooking for the troops. She'd get up every morning at 4 a.m. to cook beans, make tortillas and prepare a huge kettle of rice. She'd load everything into her handcart and push it down the highway to serve breakfast to the soldiers on the near side. Then she'd push it across the bridge – almost two kilometers, imagine! – to serve the troops on the far side. She'd get back to her hut in time to start preparing their lunch, and off she'd go again, pushing her cart."

"Very energetic, as you say, but she doesn't sound crazy."

"She was crazy," Manuel insisted, "because she only charged them for the cost of the food she cooked, and she didn't earn a penny for all that work."

"Patriotic, maybe?" Luisa ventured.

"Maybe," Manuel lifted a shoulder, "but as if that weren't enough, what did it occur to her to do after the *compas* blew up her bridge? She went out and dyed her hair red, that's what."

"Why, for heaven's sake?"

"There was a surprise attack before they blew up the bridge. The *compas* had to take out the guards at both ends so the demolition team could place the charges. But one of the *compas* was killed in the shootout, and he was carrying a plan of the defensive trenches, the location of the machinegun nests and the exact number of troops on both ends.

"A few days later a market lady warned Granny that the Guards were looking for the woman who cooked for the troops. So the dear old lady bought a packet of henna, a tube of lipstick, and went back to her ranch.

"A pair of Guards showed up the next day, asking for her. Without turning a single red hair, Granny said to them: 'Ah, that must be the old woman I rented this *finca* from last week. She threw a fit when they blew up the bridge, and she told me she was moving to San Vicente to live with her daughter.'

"'And who are you?' the Guards asked her.

"Granny drew herself up. 'I'm the respectable owner of a house of pleasure in Suchitoto,' she replied, 'but what with all these subversives shooting up the Guard barracks every other day, I ran out of clients and had to retire. That's the war for you,' she sighed."

The two of them broke out laughing.

"But that's not the end of the story," Manuel continued. "A few weeks later I was visiting a guerrilla camp near the banks of the Lempa, when whom should I see but my redheaded grandmother paddling strongly upstream in a dugout canoe filled with baskets.

103

"'I'm selling *jocotes*, papaya, lemons, sweet oranges, mangoes. Who'll buy from me?' she chanted in her street hawker's call.

"'Hello, Mama Tancho,' the camp cammander called out. Not knowing she was my grandmother, he told me: 'This is the old lady who gave us the plans for the attack on the Golden Bridge.'

"We helped her tie up the canoe under a tree, and she started complaining as soon as she hugged me:

"'Ay, Memito,' she sighed, 'these kids are making my life more difficult all the time. Ever since they blew up my bridge, I have to paddle all the way up here every day.'

"The guerrilla chief grinned and asked her: 'And what else have you brought us, Mama Tancho?'

"She removed a layer of mangoes from one of the baskets and started chanting in her streetseller's voice:

"'Fragmentation grenades, G-3 cartridges, 81-millimeter mortar rounds. Who'll buy from me?'"

PROPHESY (1)

It happened during a birthday party in Havana. The room was filled with people, tobacco smoke and noise. Suddenly, José Coronel Urtecho passed Luisa a sheet of paper on which he had written:

"You will live to see the liberation of Central America."

Luisa was so moved by the prophecy that she had the note framed and hung it in her study.

THE VOLCANOS

Izalco no longer weeps
the volcanos don't weep
no incandescent lava
flows down from their craters
waves of green
go sweeping up their flanks
beneath the greens
the *muchachos*.
Herds of Tlaloc
are the volcanos
green bulls
who graze
on the igneous rock:
Chinchontepec
Guazapa
San Miguel.
Their humps thrust up
and their skin undulates
shudders.
It's time for grazing
for storing up wrath
each pore of their skins
is a *tatú*
each pore shelters
a family
the fourteen volcanos
belong to the people
not to the Fourteen Families
to the people
they nourish their *muchachos*
conceal them
speak to them of their future

of the tangible dream
of the fiery eye
that allows no sleep
that unites all of them
holding them in suspense
whirling about them
and in the middle of night
revives their dead
with torches of light
in their hands.

THE SINGER MACHINES

Luisa had an uncle named Alfredo who never wanted to study. He was a vagabond who collected colored stones on beaches or in rock-hound fairs (he'd travel as far as Mexico sometimes to participate in an exhibit of rocks), and he also collected dirty stories.

Alfredo was madly in love with his wife, and even his brothers poked fun at him because he'd never been unfaithful to her. All of Aunt Adela's friends envied her. "You're lucky," they'd tell her. "Why don't you give us the recipe?"

His only vice was that he was a spendthrift, and they almost never had a penny. The last months had been the worst. Alfredo had lost his job after ten years working as a bank teller, because he came down with a kidney ailment and missed work too frequently. Now he was working as a Singer sewing machine salesman, and his income didn't stretch far enough. They had seven children, and even though Aunt Adela took in sewing and made tamales and sweet rolls to sell on Sundays, there was never enough money. Not many people bought Singer sewing machines.

Alfredo grew more and more worried and began suffering from insomnia. He couldn't bear seeing Adela – who was accustomed to the best of everything before her father went broke – work so hard. He had acute guilt pangs, so he spent what little money he earned on lottery tickets, but he hardly ever so much as broke even.

At last on a Monday, March 15 – he would never forget that date – Alfredo woke up lucky. Before eleven in the morning he sold two Singer machines for hard cash. Adelita is going to be so happy, he thought, I'll have to go home and tell her right away; but first I'll buy her some flowers.

He went to the market place and bought her a bunch of red roses, when his eye fell on a specialty grocery store. I'll also buy her a can of that asparagus she loves so much, he decided. And he bought two bottles of white French wine, cans of peaches and pears and tuna and caviar, and salted crackers, Dutch cheese, a bottle of whiskey and another of champagne for a candlelight celebration, chocolate bars for the children, apples, walnuts, canned apricots and a box of assorted caramels.

He had to take a taxi home, and before he entered, laden with cardboard boxes, he gave the driver a handsome tip.

The children jumped up and down around him, and Adela opened her eyes wide without understanding anything. They had a marvelous party and invited the neighbors in. When they were finally alone, drinking the champagne, Adela asked him how he had managed it. He merely kissed her and told her to enjoy the moment.

Fifteen days later the police arrived to take him away. Alfredo hadn't reappeared at the agency, and the owner wanted his Singer sewing machines back.

ALONE AGAIN

Alone again
alone
with no words
with no gestures
with no trappings
with a flavor of fruit
on our bodies
and the veil of love
uncovering us.

THE BLUE THEATRE

"I haven't been able to sleep for nights," Alejandra told Luisa. "I don't know what's wrong with me."

"Are you worried about something?"

"No, but there's a blue neon light in the street that keeps me awake. Blue," she mused. "The Blue Theatre."

Luisa and Alejandra had been friends for many years. Alejandra was Chilean, and on a number of occasions she had told Luisa about her experiences in prison after the army coup and the death of Allende, but she had never mentioned the Blue Theatre.

"What's that?" Luisa asked.

Alejandra fixed her gaze on the wall.

"It's true, I never told you about it." Her voice was expressionless. "One day while I was in prison, a guard wearing a hood came to my cell and told me to accompany him – that he was taking me to the Blue Theatre.

"'Nothing is going to happen to you,' he told me, 'all you have to do is say yes or no.'

"I began trembling," Alejandra turned her gaze to Luisa, "without knowing why. He took me into a small windowless room, illuminated with blue neon lights. Another guard, also wearing a hood, was waiting for me.

"'There is nothing to be afraid of,' he said, 'all you have to do is say yes or no when I ask you a question. Bring him in,' he ordered the first man.

"There were only two chairs covered in blue plastic. The guard sat down in one, and I was left standing. A few seconds later, two more guards in hoods entered, dragging a young man between them. At first I didn't recognize him, because his face was disfigured. Then I realized it was Sergio, a university schoolmate. He raised his eyes to look at me and shook his head imperceptibly.

111

"'Seat him there,' the guard indicated the empty chair. 'Do you know him?' he asked me.

"'No,' I said.

"'It would be better not to lie,' the guard said. 'If he's a friend of yours, I'd advise you to tell the truth. Do you know him?'

"'No,' I repeated.

"'Cut off an ear,' the interrogator ordered.

"And right there, Luisa, right before my eyes, they cut off one of his ears. I almost screamed, 'Yes, I know him,' but he raised his head again and shook it almost imperceptibly. They cut off his other ear, cut off his fingers, his hands, and he bore it without screaming. I stood there watching, looking at all that blood, looking at him. At some point I fainted and awoke in my cell. The guard told me Sergio had died, and it was my fault, because if I had said the truth they might have let him go."

THE PROCESSION

There is a still silence
thinking me
another flayed silence
walking inside me
that is wound
and scream
and destroys me
and in the middle of night
the trunk lids creak open
slowly they open
slowly
and things creep out
in Sibylline order
they creep out
and fall squirming
to the floor:
moldering dolls
unusable keys
fragments of luminous cobwebs
odors of semen
and jasmine
and decay
and the things begin to crawl
across the rug
the procession begins
to unfold
the odors
the signs
the contacts
a repressed love
forgotten smiles
and the advancing procession

is like a wave
and faces filter through
closed eyelids
and voices filter through
fragments of a sob
and vertigo
and abyss
and birdcalls screeching
– the face of my life
of my death –
and I am alone in the night
and I am afraid.

EUNICE AVILES

One time Luisa said she was an artist named Eunice Avilés, but she didn't mean to deceive.

There was a retrospective exhibit of Matisse in the Paris Museum of Modern Art, and since she loved Matisse's work she decided to spend the day there. At lunchtime, after having seen dozens of paintings she went to the cafeteria and sat down – her feet were killing her – at the only vacant table. A few minutes later, a young man who looked to be American, came up and asked if he could share the table with her.

He was, in fact, a gringo and a painter. He was enthused with the exhibit, and they began talking and exchanging opinions animatedly. After lunch they returned to the exhibit together, and Luisa suddenly found herself speaking with great self-assurance – a most unusual thing with her – about Matisse's work. She spoke with such authority that she couldn't assume the responsibility for her words.

"Are you an art professor?" the boy asked.

"A painter," Luisa fibbed without faltering.

"Why didn't you say so before? My name is Michael Stone."

"Eunice Avilés," she replied, startled at this second unnecessary lie.

"I'd love to see your paintings," Michael said enthusiastically. "Your observations and comments have fascinated me, and I'm sure I could learn a great deal from your work."

"I don't live here," Luisa said defensively, "I'm just passing through."

"Where do you live?" he asked.

"In Mikonos, in an old mill," Luisa heard herself say.

"Greece is on my itinerary, so I'll come and see you."

They continued looking at pictures and chatting animatedly. When the museum closed they went to a café near the Trocadero to have coffee.

"This has been one of the most pleasant days of my trip," Michael said, pulling out a small agenda. "Would you give me your address?"

"I have no address," Luisa laughed. "When you get to Mikonos, just ask for Eunice Avilés. It's a small island, and everybody knows my mill."

They parted with pecks on the cheek, and when Luisa had walked a few steps toward the Metro, Michael called to her: "See you soon."

Luisa started home with a preoccupied air and decided not to say a word to Bud, because he didn't like lies.

"Good grief! Why did I do that?" she asked herself as she boarded the Metro. He's probably really going to Mikonos now. What got into me, anyway? Oh well, it will be worth it. Maybe something nice will happen to him on the island, and if it hadn't been for my absurd fibs he would never have gone. Besides, who knows? He may find the Gypsy waiting for him when he arrives.

REDISCOVERING AMERICA

Finally, love
finally we settle
into a world
that is ours
it's a river
that flows
and is filled with voices
with the fertilizing presence
of the dead
with hazardous omens
with screeching birds
with forms that transform themselves
daily.
Before this it was the backwater
a drifting in suspense
a meander in the woods
where the river recoils.
Something happened suddenly
the planet sneezed
there was a floating pollen
infecting us
an intolerable
contagious pollen:
our blood raced
friends transformed
into strangers
time accelerated.
We began walking
more rapidly
made unexpected
leaps
found ourselves surrounded

by rubble
sinking into the earth
by odors of fruit
odors of dried sweat
in shirts
by plants
and children
growing
every which way
I remembered the names
of birds
the cloud colors
in the evening
the suffocating heat
the street-hawkers' cries.
This is my world,
love,
but different:
a second birth
a new world.

APPOINTMENT IN ZINICA

– For María Gertrudis

"The body was already rotting when they brought it by truck to Zinica," María Gertrudis told Luisa. "The boy had been dead for 17 days. The family opened the coffin and recognized by the teeth that it was not their son, but they didn't say anything. Their own son had gold inlays. They gave the boy a funeral with military honors, because he had died a hero's death. A group of us students who were harvesting coffee attended the funeral.

"The next day the news arrived that their own son had fallen in battle at Cuá, and the *compas* had to bury him on the battlefield at 4 in the afternoon: the same day and the same hour we had held the funeral in Zinica."

THE GYPSY (3)

"What an idiot you made of yourself the other day in the museum," the Gypsy scolded Luisa. "Poor Michael is going to arrive in Mikonos, and neither you nor I will be there. But what difference does it make to you if he suffers a disappointment? And all because you chickened out, because you didn't dare behave naturally. Why didn't you just admit that you were a frustrated artist? Any psychoanalyst would tell you that you're horribly envious of Chagall."

THE POOL

Luisa dreamt she was seated beside a pool, accompanied by her mother. The square pool had a double border, and there was a bronze statue at each corner. Luisa could see the faces of only two of the statues, because the others were hidden by foliage. The statues were of young men; one had a garland about his neck and the other a serpent.

"Take off your shoes and walk into the tank," her mother told her. "The water is magical."

Luisa obeyed. The water was tepid. She hiked her skirt above her knees and walked to the center. She wanted to see the faces of the other two statues, but she couldn't because the foliage was too thick.

"Why a garland and a serpent?" she asked.

"For humor and sorrow," her mother said. "Don't ever forget this."

And she vanished abruptly.

THE RETURN

How will the return be?
My parents won't be there
I won't climb the volcano
with them
to gather orchids.
The jasmine won't be there
nor the araucaria.
Nor will there be a fortress
in front of my house
nor children
flaunting their misery
nor mud shanties
with tin roofs.
I have never seen
my mother's tomb
my childhood
next to her
my first seedbed
of memories
my rainbow arch
glowing
dimming
sinking roots
soaring
peopling me with birds.
They were times of peace
those distant times
of somnolence
and peace.
Now is a time of war
of steps leading upward
of love that seeds dreams

and shakes one.
Return obsesses me
faces fly by
through the open fissure.
Once more there'll be peace
but of a different kind.
The rainbow glimmers
tugs at me
forcefully
not that inert peace
of shrouded eyes
it will be a rebellious
contagious peace
a peace that opens furrows
and aims at the stars.
The rainbow shatters
the sky splits open
rolls up like a scroll
of shadows
inviting us to enter
and be dazzled.
Come, love, let's return
to the future.

SALARRUE

"I hate to see him when he's wandering around on the astral plane," Celie said, "it's almost as if he were dead His body turns stiff and cold. The only thing that makes me feel easier is that he keeps on breathing, but just barely."

Salarrué, besides being a great story writer and excellent painter, also knew how to bilocate and see people's auras. He was always repeating to Luisa's mother that she had a beautiful aura.

Luisa was a close friend of his daughters, and one day, her heart in her mouth, she asked him: "What do you do in order to bilocate?"

Salarrué only laughed.

"I don't believe that you can appear in somebody else's house while you're really here all the time." Luisa squirmed with embarrassment and held her breath. She was 12 years old at the time and was passing through her scientific, materialist phase.

"Would you like me to give you a demonstration sometime?" Salarrué gave her an affectionate smile.

Luisa shook her head firmly and went out to the patio to play with her friends.

Years later, while she was combing her hair at her dressing table one night – there wasn't the slightest breeze at the time – a book suddenly fell from her bookcase onto the floor: it was Salarrué's *Cuentos de Barro*.

MANAGUA

I live instants
that alter my rhythm
that unhinge me
instants at gunpoint
awaiting the click
of the trigger
pulsation-instants
that wind me tight
the spring will snap
will shatter to bits
what happened to that other self
who wasted away
without surprises?

PLASH, PLASH, PLASH

Luisa's mother was very pious and was terrified of ghosts.

"Sometimes at night, don't you hear quick footsteps that sound as if the person were wearing floppy bedroom slippers?" she asked her daughter.

"No," Luisa replied.

"I'm the only one who hears them, but I swear I'm not crazy. They go *plash, plash, plash*, as clear as can be when they pass my bedroom door."

Years later, Etelvina, an ancient woman who had once been a nurse, came to the house to ask after Luisa's grandfather, who was very ill. As she sipped her coffee, she gazed nostalgically about the patio.

"Nobody would say it's the same house," she commented. "I used to come here more than 60 years ago, when we lived right across the street."

"Who were the owners then?" Luisa asked.

"A German and his wife, who was from Sonsonate and made delicious meringues. She never wore shoes," the old lady laughed, "but always went around in a pair of bedroom slippers that were too big for her. I still remember the *plash, plash, plash* sound she made as she walked around the house."

YOUR DEATH

Your death congeals you
you are motionless
my life in turn
flows
carrying me swiftly
toward our reunion.

NO DOGS OR MEXICANS

After graduating from high school in Santa Ana, Luisa travelled to the United States to study at a young ladies' finishing school near New Orleans. One weekend, while she was still struggling to learn English, the parents of one of her classmates invited her to accompany them to New Orleans. They were very nice to her and took her to visit the universities of Loyola and Tulane.

"It would be wonderful if you could stay on and study here," they told her. They showed her the French Quarter and took her for a boat ride on Lake Pontchartrain. Luisa was enchanted with everything.

That Sunday, before returning to school, they decided to lunch at an exclusive restaurant where they customarily went. As they sat down, Luisa noticed some signs above the bar mirror. "In God we trust; all others pay cash," she deciphered the first. The second read: "No dogs or Mexicans allowed."

"What does 'allowed' mean?" she asked her school friend. The friend explained, and Luisa started indignantly.

"Calm down, honey," the mother said soothingly, "after all, you're Salvadoran."

MORTALLY WOUNDED

When I woke up
this morning
I knew you were
mortally wounded
that I was too
that our days were numbered
our nights
that someone had counted them
without letting us know
that more than ever
I had to love you
you had to love me.
I inhaled your fragrance
I watched you sleeping
I ran the tips of my fingers
over your skin
remembered the friends
whose quota was filled
and are on the other side:
the one who died
a natural death
the one who fell in combat
the one they tortured
in jail
who kicked aside his death.
I brushed your warmth
with my lips:
mortally wounded
my love
perhaps tomorrow
and I loved you more than ever
and you loved me as well.

THE MEJIA'S DOGS

Near Aunt Lola's house in San Salvador stood the Mejía's vacant mansion in a large fruit orchard. It was protected from fruit thieves by high walls with barbed wire on top. At least 30 Great Danes lived there, and they would run about and bark all day long.

Three times a week, at 10 in the morning, a white truck stopped in front of the gate, bringing a butchered cow. The chauffeur would ring the bell, and the dogs would all start barking at once. Two men would come out through a side gate with four huge tubs to carry off the chopped-up cow that served as dogfood.

The small boys from the surrounding *mesones* would crowd about the truck, and despite the shouts and the swats that the chaffeur aimed at them, they would dart in to seize scraps of meat and offal that fell to the ground. Some would leave empty-handed, while others ran off excitedly to offer their mothers a length of intestine or a pancreas.

The dogs, inside the walls, would keep on barking desperately.

CARMEN BOMBA: POET

Luisa always felt refreshed when she remembered Carmen Bomba, the porter and human beast of burden in the Santa Ana marketplace. Each afternoon when he finished work he'd get a bit drunk to arouse his courage, and he'd pause before each open window in the neighborhood to recite the verses he had composed that day.

AUTUMN BONFIRE

And now everything is covered with smoke
my roots
my leaves
my bark
all burning in the fire
of this autumn
dying suddenly
in another body
amid a feast of flames
and murmurs.
The leaves go first
they phosphoresce a while
they fade
retreat to the bed
turn to ashes
gray clouds
that open like wings
whirl in circles
form a bed
sustain the coals
that quicken
sustain my hard bark
my roots
that glow in the center
and are not consumed
they hold the blaze
they nourish it
in the center of the fire my roots
ballerina with linked arms
a tiny gigantic salamander
it blinks
it dwindles

it unfolds
on the flaming stalk
that feeds it
my roots swim in the fire
wound my eyes
split apart
they are freedom
and death
and labyrinth
the beginning
and the end
above the clear abyss
of a bonfire
they search
tangle together
separate
explode in sparks
like an outburst of cries
and are nucleus
and memory
and tomorrow.

PROPHECY (2)

On January second, Julio telephoned from Paris to wish Luisa and Bud a happy 1984.

"I imagine you'll be coming over for the birth of your grandchild," Julio told Luisa.

"No way; it's a terribly expensive trip."

"You'll see that you'll find a way to come," he laughed, and he bade goodbye with kisses and best wishes for Nicaragua.

Six weeks later, on Sunday, February 12, Julio died in Paris. Tomás invited Luisa to accompany him to the funeral, and in the early morning of the 13th Sarah Jennifer was born.

PERSONAL CREED

I believe in my people
who have been exploited
for five hundred years
I believe in their sons
conceived in sorrow and struggle
who suffered under the Pontius Pilates
and were martyrized
sequestered
sacrificed
descended into the hell
of the *Media Luna,*
Some were resurrected
from among the dead
and returned again
to the guerrilla
they went up the mountain
and will come back
to judge their slayers.
I believe in the brotherhood of man
in the Union of Central America
in the blue cows of Chagall
in the cronopios.
I don't know if I believe
in the forgiveness
of the Squadrons of Death
but I do believe
in the resurrection of the oppressed
in the Church of the people
in the power of the people
forever and ever
Amen.

THE GYPSY (4)

"Why do you always dress in those shocking colors?"
Luisa asked the Gypsy.

"It's probably just nostalgia. When I was about 13, I
saw my life as an iridescent soap bubble. An enormous
soap bubble. But all those daily deaths, the weight of
routine, the outrageous news reports at 8 o'clock, all the
petty meanness, faded it little by little until now there
are only a few rainbow colors left."

FROM THE BRIDGE

I have freed myself at last
it has been hard to break free
almost at the end of the bridge
I pause
the water flows below
a turbulent water
sweeping fragments with it:
the voice of Carmen Lira
faces that I loved
and I passed by.
From here
from the bridge
the perspective changes
I look backward
toward the beginning:
the hesitant silhouette
of a little girl
a doll
dangling from her hand
she lets it drop
and walks toward me
she is already adolescent
gathers up her hair
and I recognize the gesture
stop, girl
stop right there
if you come any closer
it will be difficult to talk
Don Chico died
after seven operations
they let him die
in a charity hospital

they closed Ricardo's college
and he died as well
during the earthquake
his heart failed.
Do you remember the massacre
that left Izalco without menfolk?
You were seven years old.
How can I explain it to you
nothing has changed
and they keep killing people daily.
It's better if you stop there
I remember you well at that age
you wrote honeyed poems
were horrified by violence
taught the neighborhood children
to read.
What would you say
if I told you that Pedro
your best student
rotted away in jail
and that Sarita
the little blue-eyed girl
who made up stories
let herself be seduced
by the eldest son
of her employers
and afterwards she sold herself
for twenty-five cents?
You've taken another step
you wear your hair short
have textbooks under your arm
poor deluded creature
you learned the consolations
of philosophy
before understanding
why you had to be consoled

your books spoke to you
of justice
and carefully omitted
the injustice
that has always surrounded us
you went on with your verses
searched for order in chaos
and that was your goal
or perhaps your condemnation.
You are coming closer now
your arms filled with children
it is easy to distract yourself
with a mother's role
and shrink the world
to a household.
Stop there
don't come any closer
you still wouldn't recognize me
you still have to undergo
the deaths of Roque
of Rodolfo
all those innumerable deaths
that assail you
pursue you
define you
in order to dress in these feathers
(my feathers of mourning)
to peer out
through these pitiless
scrutinizing eyes
to have my claws
and this sharp beak.
I never found the order
I searched for
but always a sinister
and well-planned disorder

that increases in the hands
of those who hold power
while the others
who clamor for
a more kindly world
a world with less hunger
and more hopefulness
die of torture
in the prisons.
Don't come any closer
there's a stench of carrion
surrounding me.

FINAL ACT

Luisa dreamt that she entered a theatre accompanied by a little girl. The theatre was semi-circular in form, and she saw her uncle Ricardo beckoning to her from one of the back rows. She led the little girl by the hand to where he was, and the two of them sat down beside him.

The stage was filled with cribs. Suddenly Luisa saw herself walking among them. All the cribs were occupied by little girls, some recently born and others as old as five. They were all crying loudly. Even those who were asleep were crying. Luisa comforted them, one by one. When she had made the round of all the cribs, she sat down in the center of the stage and began telling stories to distract them.

The scene changed. Now it was the grand salon of a Renaissance palace. Luisa saw herself seated on an ornate chair. Two pages dressed in white stood guard at the entrance. Ocho, the small Dachshund she had owned in Mallorca and who looked very much like Cuis, came over to her and, with difficulty, jumped up on her lap. Luisa started petting her, scratching her ears and begging her for forgiveness for having had her spayed so she could never have puppies.

The theatre went dark. When the lights came on again, Ricardo was no longer there. Luisa got up to leave, but the little girl insisted that she wanted to see more.

"The play is over," Luisa assured her, "and all the people have left."

They started climbing the steps, Luisa holding the girl's hand. Halfway up the stairs Luisa realized that the little girl had been transformed into a rag doll, that she was clutching the hand of a lifeless rag doll.

141

THE CARTOGRAPHY OF MEMORY

I

Not yet
I can't go back yet
I am still forbidden
to plunge into your roads
to yield to your rivers
to contemplate your volcanos
to rest in the shade
of my ceiba.
From abroad I see you
my heart watches you
from abroad,
constricted, watches you
in memories
between wavering bars
of memory
that widen
and close
ebb and flow in my tears.
It is difficult to sing you
from exile
difficult to celebrate
your nebulous
jagged map.
I can't do it yet
a dry sob
sticks in my throat.
It is difficult to sing you
when a heavy boot

with foreign hobnails
tears and cleaves
your flesh.

II

This morning
in the mail
a child's drawing:
black trees
withered branches
heads dangling
like seedpods.
"A refugee child,"
Rosa says in her letter
the skull facing me
is winking one eye.
The child knows it all
guesses it
five hundred years ago
Malinche
handed the invader
her continent
handed it over out of love
out of madness.
He always knew it
knew it yesterday
when he watched
his father's head fall
while trying
to tell him something.
Treacherous Malinche
the blossoms of her love
dropped away

and there remained heads
dangling like seedpods.
Fifty years ago
the bewitched tree
(the Indian girl repented
and embraced it weeping)
again produced
a harvest of skulls
Izalco wept
dry tears
and the country mourned.
The most recent harvest
has been the richest:
children
girls
men
the people's red blood
exploding in the air.
The malinche tree is perfidious
the Indian girl baptized it
bewitched it.
The child knows it all
he senses it
his last glimpse
as he flees:
the doors and windows
half-open
the marauding soldiers
among the black trees.
He always knew it
ever since yesterday
drops of blood
are the fallen petals
and from the branches
dangle heads
like seedpods.

III

The terrain in my country
is abrupt
the gullies go dry
in the summertime
and are stained with red
in the winter.
The Sumpul is boiling with corpses
a mother said
the Goascarán
the Lempa
all are boiling with the dead.
The rivers no longer sing
they lament
they sweep their dead along
cradle them
they twinkle
under the tepid moon
under the dark
accomplice night
they cradle their dead
the wounded
those who are fleeing
those who pass by
they grow irate
bubbling and seething
dawn draws near
almost within reach
the rivers are coffins
crystalline flasks
cradling their dead
escorting them
between their wide banks
the dead sail down

and the sea receives them
and they revive.

IV

How was my ceiba
the one facing the park
the one to which
I made a promise?
I remember it
as a shadowed roof
as a gigantic pillar
sustaining the sky
as the sentinel
of my childhood.
Beneath its thick branches
each of them like a trunk
the street sellers
rested
children and dogs
scampered about
the air paused
to watch us.
My absences
have been lengthy
innumerable
lengthy
but they never weighed on me
like now.
I still must return
the final station
is always the hardest
weariness accumulates

dismembers us.
How was my ceiba?
I sense your map
in its foliage
the circle is open
I must still return
to close it
the trunk of the ceiba
is thick
cannot be encircled
with an embrace
I have made many trips
around it
many slow circles.
They won't let me return.
Hostile forces
forbid it.
Just one last circle
to close the ritual
one last return
to arrive at my Kaaba
and sit in the park
to contemplate it.

V

They wanted to flatten El Salvador.
With heavy bulldozers
they ripped through your hills
steamrolled your soil
tore into a crust
of your history.
Strange plants

began sprouting
from the rocks they sprouted
from the cut banks
of the highway.
Someone spread the alarm
called in biologists
the regime's academicians
and foreign observors.
Since the Jurassic age
they affirmed
these types of plants
had never been seen
in the country.
This one is called Liberty
said the oldest wise man
this other one Justice
and that one over there
is Conscience.
The bulldozer returned
to uproot them.
The plants grew stronger
the guerrillas began
to flourish
the plants spread
along with the combats
the *muchachos* cover their heads
with the widest
most lustrous leaves:
long columns of ants
advancing toward the sun.
Airplanes don't see them
can't detect them
the bulldozers keep on
crushing rocks
opening highways
the seeds

were awaiting their chance
for milennia
the plants proliferated,
the guerrillas
more advisers
arrive
to consult with each other.
The muchachos
the plants
climb toward the future
toward the sun.

VI

Izalco no longer weeps
the volcanos don't weep
no incandescent lava
flows down from their craters
waves of green
go sweeping up their flanks
beneath the greens
the *muchachos*.
Herds of Tlaloc
are the volcanos
green bulls
who graze
on the igneous rock:
Chinchontepec
Guazapa
San Miguel.
Their humps thrust up
and their skin undulates
shudders.

149

It's time for grazing
for storing up wrath
each pore of their skins
is a *tatú*
each pore shelters
a family
the fourteen volcanos
belong to the people
not to the Fourteen Families
to the people
they nourish their *muchachos*
conceal them
speak to them of their future
of the tangible dream
of the fiery eye
that allows no sleep
that unites all of them
holding them in suspense
whirling about them
and in the middle of night
revives their dead
with torches of light
in their hands.

VII

How will the return be?
My parents won't be there
I won't climb the volcano
with them
to gather orchids.
The jasmine won't be there
nor the araucaria.

Nor will there be a fortress
in front of my house
nor children
flaunting their misery
nor mud shanties
with tin roofs.
I have never seen
my mother's tomb
my childhood
next to her
my first seedbed
of memories
my rainbow arch
glowing
dimming
sinking roots
soaring
peopling me with birds.
They were times of peace
those distant times
of somnolence
and peace.
Now is a time of war
of steps leading upward
of love that seeds dreams
and shakes one.
Return obsesses me
faces fly by
through the open fissure.
Once more there'll be peace
but of a different kind.
The rainbow glimmers
tugs at me
forcefully
not that inert peace
of shrouded eyes

it will be a rebellious
contagious peace
a peace that opens furrows
and aims at the stars.
The rainbow shatters
the sky splits open
rolls up like a scroll
of shadows
inviting us to enter
and be dazzled.
Come, love, let's return
to the future.

Claribel Alegría was born in Estelí, Nicaragua, on 12 May 1924, but considers herself Salvadoran insofar as she moved to Santa Ana, El Salvador, at a very early age, where she grew up. She earned her B.A. degree in philosophy and letters at George Washington University, Washington, D.C. She and her husband have lived in various Latin American and European countries for the past 35 years. During recent years they have divided their time between Mallorca, Spain, and Managua, Nicaragua.

In her writing and in her personal life, Claribel Alegría has for many years been an outspoken advocate of the liberation struggle in her home, El Salvador, and her region, Central America. She has published 10 volumes of poetry, three short novels and a book of children's stories. In collaboration with her husband, the U.S. writer Darwin J. Flakoll, she has published a novel, several books of testimony and contemporary Latin American history, as well as a number of anthologies. In 1978 her book of poems, *Sobrevivo*, won the Casa de las Americas Prize of Cuba.

OTHER CURBSTONE PRESS TITLES
BY LATIN AMERICAN WRITERS:

poetry:

DE REPENTE/ALL OF A SUDDEN, Teresa de Jesús (pseud.),
trans. by Maria A. Proser & James Scully. bilingual. 2nd
printing. 0-915306-14-X. $7.50 pa.

LET'S GO!, Otto René Castillo, trans. by Margaret Randall.
bilingual. 0-915306-44-1. $7.50 pa.

QUECHUA PEOPLES POETRY, trans. by Maria A. Proser, Arlene
Scully & James Scully. 2nd printing. 0-915306-09-3. $7.50 pa.

POEMS, by Roque Dalton, trans. by Richard Schaaf. 0-915306-
45-X. $13.50 cl. / 0-915306-43-3. $7.50 pa.

THE EARTH IS A SATELLITE OF THE MOON, by Leonel
Rugama, trans. by Sara Miles, Richard Schaaf & Nancy
Weisberg. 0-915306-54-9. $15.95 cl. / 0-915306-50-6. $9.00 pa.

CAMOURADE, Selected Poems of Paul Laraque, translated by
Rosemary Manno. bilingual. 0-915306-71-9. $9.95 pa.

nonfiction:

MIGUEL MARMOL, by Roque Dalton, trans. by Kathleen Ross &
Richard Schaaf. 0-915306-68-9. $19.95 cl. (Also available in a
limited edition of 100 copies signed by Miguel Mármol: $64.95 .)

TESTIMONY: Death of a Guatemalan Village, by Victor Montejo,
trans. by Victor Perera. 0-915306-61-1. $16.95 cl. / 0-915306-
65-4. $8.95 pa.

this first English language edition
of
LUISA IN REALITYLAND
by
Claribel Alegría

translated by
Darwin J. Flakoll

is printed on acid-free paper
in an edition of
2500 copies
by
Curbstone Press

of which
100 numbered copies
are signed by
the author and the translator

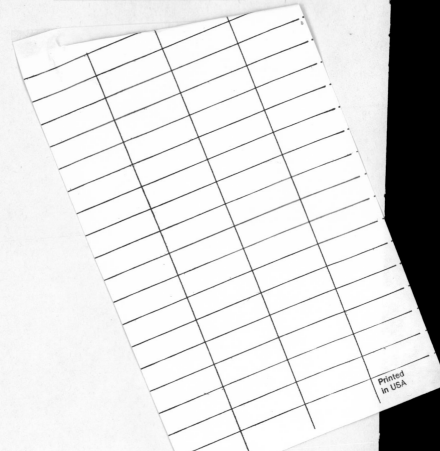

Printed
in USA